The day seemed near perfect

As they walked in silence, Hannah's gaze followed the dance of sunshine through the branches. She was mesmerized by the dappled design shimmering on the grass.

"Thanks for inviting me," she said, breaking the quiet. "I'm usually not comfortable with strangers."

Andrew slid his arm about her shoulder. "Were you always shy?"

His gentle touch surprised her. "I'm not really shy," Hannah said, immediately realizing she'd opened a door she preferred to keep closed.

"So what is it then?"

"It's the way I was brought up." She hoped the explanation would suffice. And yet, when she looked into Andrew's eyes, she felt a nudge to be honest. If her background was going to chase him away, then she'd better reveal it now before she had too much at stake in their friendship.

Books by Gail Gaymer Martin

Love Inspired

Upon a Midnight Clear #117
Secrets of the Heart #147
A Love for Safekeeping #161
*Loving Treasures #177
*Loving Hearts #199
Easter Blessings #202
  "The Butterfly Garden"
The Harvest #223
  "All Good Gifts"
*Loving Ways #231
*Loving Care #239
Adam's Promise #259
*Loving Promises #291
*Loving Feelings #303
*Loving Tenderness #323

*Loving

Steeple Hill Books

The Christmas Kite
That Christmas Feeling
  "Christmas Moon"

GAIL GAYMER MARTIN

When not behind her computer, Gail enjoys a busy life—traveling, especially to present workshops at conferences, and speaking at churches, business groups and civic events. She sings with the Detroit Lutheran Singers. She lives with her amazingly wonderful husband in Lathrup Village, Michigan. Gail praises God for the gift of writing. It is a career she never dreamed possible. She has written over thirty works of fiction and a number of nonfiction titles.

Her novels have been finalists for numerous awards, and she won the Holt Medallion 2001 and 2003, the Texas Winter Rose 2003, the American Christian Romance Writers 2002 Book of the Year Award and *Romantic Times* Reviewers' Choice Best Love Inspired novel of 2002 with *A Love for Safekeeping*. Gail loves to hear from her readers. Write to her at P.O. Box 760063, Lathrup Village, MI, 48076 or visit her Web site at www.gailmartin.com.

LOVING TENDERNESS

GAIL GAYMER MARTIN

Steeple
Hill®

Published by Steeple Hill Books™

STEEPLE HILL BOOKS

**Steeple
Hill**®

ISBN 0-373-87333-6

LOVING TENDERNESS

Copyright © 2005 by Gail Gaymer Martin

www.SteepleHill.com

Printed in U.S.A.

Let brotherly love continue. Be not forgetful to entertain strangers: for thereby some have entertained angels unawares.

—*Hebrews* 13:1-2

Thanks to my faithful readers. An author's greatest pleasure is to write stories you love, stories that touch your hearts and lives. You've been so kind and supportive in your letters and e-mails. Many have sent gifts and shared your lives and talents with me. Thanks from the bottom of my heart.

Thank you also to The Haven with locations throughout the Detroit metropolitan area, and to Sue Palmer and Margaret Waddell from the Christian Women's Center in Georgia for providing me with information about shelter programs.

Chapter One

Andrew Somerville's headlights caught something moving along the shoulder ahead of him, and he leaned forward to make out the silhouette. A driver in distress, he figured as he slowed.

Hypnotized by the swish-swish of his windshield wipers, he peered through the early April downpour. A yawn escaped him, and he lifted his hand to cover his mouth, then drew back his shoulders, hoping to relieve the tension he'd felt ever since returning months earlier to Loving. Loving, a town he'd once called home. Despite the town's acceptance, he now felt like an outsider.

A frown tightened his forehead as he rolled past, observing the silhouette of a woman gripping the hand of a small child. Their coats were sodden in the midnight deluge. Without hesitation, he pulled onto the shoulder ahead of them. His curiosity grew as he observed them through the rearview mirror.

After he'd stopped, the woman seemed to hesitate and drew the child to her. She didn't step closer but waited for him to make a move.

Andrew opened his car door and stuck his head into the driving torrent. "Can I help you?"

A clap of thunder covered his voice, and the woman tilted her ear toward him, letting him know she hadn't heard.

He ignored the downpour and stepped onto the shoulder. "Do you need help? Can I give you a lift?" His vision blurred as raindrops streamed past his eyes.

She looked down at the child clinging to her pant leg as if weighing her options. "Do I know you?"

"No. I live in Loving. Andrew Somerville."

She moved closer, her eyes probing his as she tried to place him. "I know your name."

Andrew beckoned her. "Then climb in. I'll give you a ride into town."

She headed for his sedan, looking as weighed down as the soggy clothes she wore.

Drenched now, Andrew slipped back into the driver's seat and leaned over to push open the passenger door. The child began to climb in, his eyes glazed with exhaustion and confusion, but when the woman realized the car had bucket seats, she opened the back door and motioned the child inside, then slid in beside him.

In the dim overhead light, Andrew winced, seeing a nasty bruise marring her cheek and a bloodied cut on her lip. Automobile accident? He felt his scowl deepen as he tried to recall an abandoned car on the road behind him, but he'd seen nothing.

"Thanks," she said, pulling the door closed. "I'm sorry. We're getting your seats wet."

His seats seemed the least of her problems. "Don't worry about it," he said, then listened to the click of the seat belts before he shifted into gear and rolled out onto the highway.

"Where's your car?" he asked, glancing over his shoulder.

She didn't respond.

A silent chill filled the air, and he studied her through the rearview mirror, curious as to what had stopped her from answering. She was an attractive woman despite the bruises and her wet hair plastered against her scalp.

"It's a personal problem," she said, finally, her eyes narrowing when she saw his frown in the mirror.

The comment made him more inquisitive, but he stopped that line of questioning. "Where are you headed?"

"I'm tired, Mom," the boy whimpered.

"Be patient, JJ. We'll be somewhere soon."

In the mirror, Andrew saw the child snuggle closer to her side. The boy looked about school age, maybe younger, and Andrew noticed for the first time that he was dressed in pajamas beneath his jacket. His bewilderment turned to concern, and she still hadn't answered his question.

"Where are you headed?" he asked once more.

"I—I'm not sure."

He heard a tremor in her voice, and his mind sailed back to days when he didn't know where he would spend the night, either. "Are you in some kind of trouble?"

She responded with silence, then a lengthy sigh. "It's difficult to talk now."

Through the mirror, he saw her head tilt toward the child. The boy seemed to be nearly asleep, and that comment as well as her bruised face gave him an answer.

"Husband problems. I'm sorry."

She glanced toward JJ. "He's not my husband. He's my ex."

Ex. Divorced. Her comment stopped Andrew cold, and he felt his mouth tighten at her brusque statement.

"I see," he said. "Then how about the shelter?"

"Yes, that will do," she said, her voice heavy with resignation.

"They'll treat you well there. Some of us from the church do volunteer work for them. It's been a wonderful experience for me," Andrew said, shifting the subject to something more positive.

She fell silent for a moment, and when she spoke, her voice seemed to come from miles away. "You don't need to hear my problems."

"We've all had them," he said, assuming she'd heard about his. He gave her another glance in the mirror. "You're related to Philip Somerville. Everyone's heard of him."

"He's my older brother."

"I'm Hannah Currey."

Andrew realized his name meant nothing to her. Or if it did, her voice hadn't registered it.

She drew the boy closer. "This is my son, JJ."

"Hi, JJ," Andrew said, hoping to break through the child's fear. "It's kind of late for a young man to be out in his pajamas. I'm glad I can give you a lift." He tried to make his tone upbeat, but he didn't feel lighthearted. The memories took him back to his troubled years and his fall from grace. Regret shot through him, realizing what pride and arrogance had done to his life.

"I could go to a motel," Hannah said, "but I left without money, and I don't know when I can..." Her voice faded as if she realized she'd said too much.

"I'd be happy to give you a loan," he said, surprised as the words left his mouth.

"No. Thanks. I have a job. I can sort things out tomorrow."

Tomorrow. The uplifting Broadway song from the musical *Annie* raced through his mind as he looked at the storm beating against his windshield. He hoped the sun would come out tomorrow for her, and for himself for that matter. "Where do you work?"

"Loving Hair Salon. I'm a shampooer."

Earning a living as a shampooer didn't leave much money for luxuries, he guessed. Yet as he looked at her through his mirror, he noted the determination on her face. He hoped the expression wasn't just hiding insecurity. Years ago he'd learned to put on a mask of confidence.

He turned down Washington Street and headed toward Loving Arms. "The shelter belonged to the Hartmann sisters. They ran a rooming house with the same name. Maybe you know them." He looked into the rearview mirror and saw her shake her head.

Andrew pulled to the curb and felt for his umbrella in the storage pocket on his door. He pulled it out, then had another thought. He dug into his pocket, located a business card, and handed it to her across the back seat. "If you ever need anything, please let me know."

Hannah stared at the small card and slipped it into her shoulder bag. "Thanks," she said, but she sounded skeptical.

As Andrew leaned across the seat rest, he noticed the boy had fallen asleep. "Here's my umbrella." He extended it over the seat. "If you hold it, I'll carry your son up to the door."

She ignored his offer. "No, don't trouble yourself. I

can carry him." She pulled her purse onto her shoulder, then pushed against the door.

Andrew disregarded her refusal. He slid from the seat and hurried around to shield her from the rain. He had to admire her, beaten and bruised, yet determined to survive.

The storm had lessened, but a steady rain continued to fall, and the curb gutter had flooded with water. When he reached her side, he held the umbrella above her head as she climbed out and hoisted the boy into her arms. He'd thought her determined, but now stubborn seemed more accurate.

"Thanks so much. I'm sorry about the wet seats." She pushed the door closed with her shoulder and stepped away before he could act.

Her apology astounded him. He held the umbrella over her as she made her way up the sidewalk and climbed the stairs to the broad porch. Once under its cover, she stopped. "I don't want to keep you. Thanks again."

This time he took the hint and backed away, wishing she had taken the umbrella. He could have returned tomorrow to retrieve it. He realized he wanted to learn more about the woman and boy. She intrigued him beyond reason.

The bruise and bloodied lip clung to his thoughts as he made his way back to the car. Out of the rain, he waited while she pushed the bell, and when the porch light finally snapped on, he shifted into Drive and pulled away.

Hannah frowned as the porch light suddenly flashed in her eyes, and a shiver prickled through her from the cold night air against her damp clothing. She'd never thought it would come to this—a shelter for abused women.

She had made it on her own and protected her son, but tonight she'd been degraded for the last time by the man she'd once vowed to love until death parted them. He'd deceived her in so many ways, and she wondered how she had been so gullible. Her stomach turned at the memories.

Hannah watched a shadowy figure move behind the curtained window and shifted JJ's weight in her arms as she waited. The door slipped open a notch while a chain latch controlled the gap.

Tired eyes studied her through the opening. "Can I help you?" the woman asked.

"I need a place to stay," Hannah said, finding it difficult to say the words.

The woman shifted her sleepy gaze to JJ, then to Hannah's battered face. "One minute." She brushed strands of gray hair from her cheek and closed the door.

Hannah heard the rattle of the chain before the knob turned and the woman opened the door fully.

"Come in," she said, stepping back as Hannah entered. "I'm Lucy Dagan, the night manager. I'm glad you found us." She closed the door and locked it, then turned back and motioned toward a hallway. "Let me show you to a room." She tugged her robe around her frame and retied the sash.

"I'm Hannah," Hannah said as she hoisted JJ into her arms more securely and followed Lucy down a hallway beyond the open staircase. Lucy opened the second door and turned on the light. "While you get him undressed, I'll find some clothes for you both. What size does your boy wear?"

"JJ's a size four," Hannah said, frustrated she hadn't at least taken some of their clothing from the house, but escaping had been her only thought and packing would have awakened Jack.

Lucy disappeared for a moment and returned with two towels, then vanished again into the hallway.

Hannah bent over her son, pulling off his soggy garments and drying him off while her mind sorted through the horror of Jack's intrusion a few hours earlier. Yet as the vision threatened to fill her mind, the kindness of Andrew Somerville covered it. She'd been frightened when he'd pulled onto the shoulder until it dawned on her that the man's car was white and Jack's was deep blue. She'd feared Jack had awakened and followed her, ready to beat her again for running away. Her hands trembled while the memory swept over her.

As she straightened, Lucy returned with an armful of clothing. "Try these," she said, dropping the garments onto the bed. "Hopefully you can find something there for tonight and the morning. Tomorrow you're welcome to go through our wardrobes and find whatever you need."

"You're very kind," Hannah said, wishing she was home in her cozy bed—at least, what had once been her cozy bed.

"I'll let you be," Lucy said, backing toward the door. "It's late, but if you need anything, just let me know, I'm right next door." She stepped into the hallway, then halted. "The bathroom's across the hall." She gestured toward the doorway. "Good night."

Hannah said good night, and when the woman had gone, she tucked JJ into the bed. Then she sank onto the edge of the mattress and buried her throbbing face in her hands. She felt violated, dirty, empty. What had happened to the God of mercy and loving kindness that the Bible spoke of? She'd believed once, but Jack's violation of her home and of her had been another example proving that God's plan didn't take her into account.

She brushed the angry tears from her eyes and picked through the clothing Lucy had given her. A faded nightgown slipped from beneath the stack, and she lifted it. Too large, but it would do. She laid the other garments on a chair in the small room and stepped into the corridor.

The bathroom door stood ajar, and she pushed it open and went inside. The light flashed across her face as she flicked the switch, and Hannah felt startled to see the dazed look in her eyes, the sunken, pale face that stared back at her, cheek darkened by a large bruise. She touched her lip and winced at the sting of the wound. Blood had dried, and beneath it, she felt the swelling.

Hannah locked the door and slipped out of her sodden clothing. She pushed back the plastic shower curtain. The old-fashioned tub on clawed feet looked clean and had been supplied with soap and shampoo. She took a washcloth from the stack and turned on the tap. Cool water ran across her hand until the temperature finally rose, and she stepped into the tub and the cleansing water.

The heat struck her chilled skin and burned, but she didn't care. She lathered her body, scrubbing away the soil and trying to scrub away the feeling of Jack's hands. The bruise on her cheek smarted as she soaped her face, and for the first time, she saw the dark contusions on her arms from Jack's fingers. *Oh Lord, why? If I only understood.*

Salty tears mingled with the water as she shampooed her hair, fighting the visions that assailed her behind her closed eyes. She rinsed the soap from her hair and body, searching for answers. What could she do now to protect herself? She'd divorced Jack because of his abuse, a divorce that had wounded her deeply. She'd grown up believing that marriage was a promise to God, but then God had promised to love her and care for her, and He hadn't seemed to be holding up His part of the bargain, either.

Divorce hadn't helped. Jack harassed her on the phone. He'd come to her apartment, and she knew he'd followed her on occasion. She had nothing to offer him. The love she'd had for him had died little by little with each slap, each punch. She couldn't take a chance. If he slapped her around, he would soon abuse their son. Divorce might be against God's will, but allowing her son to be battered seemed worse.

Clean, but not feeling wholly cleansed, Hannah turned off the tap, grabbed a towel, and dried herself while her mind raced with questions. She needed safety and comfort. She needed protection from Jack. Tonight the shelter would provide that, but what about tomorrow and next week and the week after that?

Loving Arms. The name wrapped around her. That's what she needed—loving arms to hold her close and guard her against hurt and evil. Her mind flew back to her childhood days and a picture book her mother had given her. It was filled with stories of Jesus, and she recalled the one where Jesus stood with his arms open to the children. Today she wanted to be that child, wrapped in Jesus's loving arms. Anger tore through her instead, as she envisioned God's arms folded tightly across His chest, unwelcoming. He hadn't opened them to her. What had she done for God to forsake her?

Hannah made her way back to the bedroom and

crawled in beside JJ. He shifted as she settled in, and she touched his warm, relaxed hand, thankful that he hadn't seen what had happened. She'd pulled him from sleep to make their escape.

She rolled on her side and closed her eyes, longing to fall asleep and awaken to find it had been a bad dream.

In the morning when Hannah opened her eyes to the strange surroundings, the night's events crashed down around her, and she knew it hadn't been a dream at all.

Seeing JJ's chest still rising and falling in deep slumber, she gazed at him a moment, seeing his brown curly hair pressed against his head by beads of perspiration. He looked so innocent. Hannah inched her legs over the edge of the bed so as not to disturb him and gathered her thoughts.

During the night her anger had given way to resentment. She'd been able to stand on her own after Jack left, and Hannah loved her independence. It gave her pride to provide a home and support for her son. Now she felt displaced.

In a few weeks, she would begin a better-paying job, one that could give them a few luxuries. *Work?* This morning, the word filled her with questions. If she worked today, she would have to worry about Jack showing up at the salon. Plus, Jack had hidden her keys so she'd left her car at the apartment. Though she had extra keys somewhere, she needed to find them, and now she feared returning for them.

And their clothes. Hannah thought about her closets at home and wondered when she could go back inside. She eyed the pile of garments on the chair where she'd dropped them the night before. She rummaged through the stack until she found a pair of slacks and a top that looked as though they might fit.

The scent of coffee drifted beneath the bedroom door. She didn't like being beholden to anyone, but it was temporary, and she appreciated the help. One bright memory was the man who picked them up on the road—Philip Somerville's brother Andrew. He made her curious. The Somervilles knew nothing about poverty or hardship. They'd lived in the lap of luxury all their lives. Yet he'd stopped to give her a ride. Perhaps it was his good deed for the day, but she appreciated his kindness.

In the bathroom, Hannah brushed her teeth and faced the mirror. She looked worse than she had the night before. The bruise had darkened to a deep purple edged with sickly green. She lifted her chin. Jack could hurt her body, but he couldn't destroy her spirit.

Though she'd washed the blood from her lip the night before, her lip remained swollen. She dug into her purse for lipstick and dragged the tube of coral across her mouth, wincing at the pressure. Internal scars could be hidden—she'd lived that way much of her life—but the outer ones were a visual reminder of Jack's rage. He'd tried to bring her down before, but he'd failed. He would fail again. Hannah would come out the winner.

Andrew straightened his tie as he neared his office at Bay Breeze Resort. He felt weary and rattled as he covered a yawn. He'd awakened before sunrise—not awakened really, because he hadn't really slept at all, thinking of the woman and child. So he'd risen and come to work. Even at this early hour, seeing eager guests at breakfast or already outside in the cool morning sunshine wearing jackets and coats surprised him.

He stepped into the lobby. He had always admired his father's vision of the hotel and all that it offered—tennis courts, golf, gardens, fine dining and well-appointed rooms. During the seven years Andrew had been gone, his father had died and Philip had taken over the reins. Under Philip's guidance, the resort had blossomed and now offered sailing and many other amenities that helped make it one of the finest resorts in the area.

The memory of the years he'd been gone clouded Andrew's thoughts. He'd walked away, left the family home and business to strike out on his own. He'd taken his share of his inheritance and headed into a world that failed him. No, he'd failed, and that was what had hurt so badly. Then he'd been too ashamed to come home, needy and empty. The experience raked at his pride and self-worth.

The thing that hurt the most had been—

"Andrew."

Hearing his brother's voice, Andrew turned. "What are you doing here?"

"Just visiting. We haven't seen you lately, and I wondered how things are going. Ian said he's turning the resort over to you while he and his family go on vacation. A well-deserved one, I might add."

Andrew studied his brother's face. Did Philip doubt he could handle the manager's job? Ian Barry would only be gone two weeks. Andrew felt certain he could deal with the resort details for that short time, but— He stopped his negative thoughts. "I said I'd manage the place for the fortnight, unless you have some reservations."

"Reservations?" Philip's forehead wrinkled as a frown settled over his face. "No. I think it's a great idea. You know the business backward and forward. If I hadn't given the manager's job to Ian before you returned home, I'd have given it to you happily. You know that."

Insecurity clawed at Andrew. "Thanks for your confidence, but I've been away a long time. You've made a lot of changes."

"Yes, but you've been back for a few months now. It's not that different. The marina is the biggest change, but we have staff who know that business."

Philip had a knack for hiring quality people. He'd been a workaholic for years, just like his father. That's why Andrew had left. He hadn't been able to compete with them, and he'd hoped being on his own would help him find his own niche and prove his worth. Unfortunately, he hadn't succeeded.

"So what about dropping by for dinner?" Philip asked. "Ellie misses you, and since Jemma's due in another month, she won't be up for preparing you a home-cooked meal after the baby comes. You don't want to settle for my cooking, do you?"

Andrew grinned, knowing cooking wasn't one of his brother's talents. He envisioned Philip's wife Jemma, a woman filled with grace and charm who'd made Philip a new man.

When Andrew had returned to town, he'd spotted her rounded belly and, surprising himself, envied Philip's fatherhood. Three-year-old Ellie, as sunny as her mother, couldn't help but make him smile. "How about Friday night?"

"Friday it is. We'll see you then," Philip said. He squeezed Andrew's shoulder and headed toward the registration desk.

Andrew watched him for a moment, then turned toward the broad expanse of lobby windows that looked out onto Lake Michigan. Along the sidewalk, he saw a young woman and boy walking hand in hand—mother and son, he guessed, and his mind slipped back to the evening before.

Hannah and JJ had filled his mind as he tried to sleep, and he still couldn't shake the image of their drenched forms the night before. Their lives had been upset by something brutal, so unlike the carefree young woman and child he now observed through the window. As he watched, the young woman prodded the boy, and he ran forward into the arms of a man—his father probably. The woman joined them, and they walked arm in arm down the path toward the lake's sparkling water—a happy family.

A sunshiny lake had not been what greeted Hannah on this bright morning, Andrew knew. She'd probably awakened in a barren room inside the Loving Arms Women's Shelter. His stomach tightened as he recalled awakening in one too many barren hotel rooms himself after too many drinks had blurred his thoughts and drowned out his failures.

He'd never been a drinker before he left home, but somehow, his life had changed from a walk with God to a walk with sin. He'd wallowed away his days on speculative business deals and eager women looking for a man with money. Now nothing seemed to relieve him from those painful recollections.

Andrew turned away from the window and shifted direction toward the restaurant. He would make sure everything was running as smooth as their chocolate silk pie, and then he hoped to slip out and make a quick trip to Loving Arms to check on Hannah. He sensed she needed help, and he wanted to offer his assistance.

As the plan began forming in his mind, he recalled her insistence on lugging JJ up the porch stairs without his aid. He pictured the determination on her face. Maybe what he now sensed was his own need and not Hannah's at all.

Chapter Two

Hannah lowered the telephone receiver and leaned against the hall stand. Missing work hadn't been her preference, but Lucy had insisted, saying she needed to get her thoughts and possessions together. Their clothing was at the apartment, and she needed to retrieve it, along with her car. JJ needed to have his own toys, too. She wanted to protect JJ from any more upheaval than necessary.

She shook her head and returned to the kitchen, eyeing her half-empty coffee cup. The contents felt cold to the touch, and she headed to the pot to warm it. Except for Lucy, she hadn't heard a soul that morning and it was already nine. Lucy had popped into the kitchen earlier to say she'd spent the morning filling out report forms and would be leaving as soon as her replacement arrived.

Irritation skittered up Hannah's back. She wanted to leave, but she felt bound to the shelter. Though she tried to block the thought, she couldn't help wondering if Jack had been driving the streets looking for her. Jack's violence preoccupied her. She'd done everything she could to stop his ranting. In Proverbs, God said a gentle answer turns away wrath, but it hadn't worked on Jack. Nothing had.

Hannah looked up when she heard Lucy.

"I'll be leaving now," Lucy said, slipping on her coat.

"Thanks again for your help last night," Hannah said, truly grateful the woman had answered the door.

"That's what I'm here for. I'll see you tonight." Lucy gestured behind her. "I'm leaving you in good hands."

As she said those words, another woman appeared in the doorway. "Hi," she said, stepping forward and extending her hand. "I'm Annie Dewitt. I live next door."

Her comment confused Hannah. She glanced at Lucy, then back to the attractive blond woman. "You're a neighbor? At first I thought you worked here."

"I do. It's very convenient living next door."

Hannah felt a smile rise to her face, and the grin stretched her swollen skin. She rose and accepted the woman's hand in a firm, amiable shake. Hannah liked her immediately. Her direct look and her smile made Hannah feel more at ease than she'd felt since she'd left her apartment in the middle of the night.

Lucy waved goodbye, leaving her alone with Annie who'd headed for the coffeemaker. Before Hannah returned to her seat, she strode to the doorway and listened for sounds of JJ stirring. She heard nothing.

When she turned, Annie had poured a cup of coffee and settled onto a chair.

"Where are the others?" Hannah asked, joining her.

Annie's brows lifted in question. "Staff, you mean?"

"No. Other women. Children."

"You're alone today. People come and go. Once they feel safe again, they return home or sometimes move in with family for a while. Security and independence are what we want for our families, and we do everything we can to empower them."

That's what Hannah wanted—security and independence, without fear of Jack's threats.

Annie took another sip, then lowered the coffee cup to the table. "You have a son, Lucy tells me."

"Yes. JJ. He's four and a half." She gestured toward the hallway. "He's still sleeping. It was late when we left home." Her heart lurched at the memory. "Jack hasn't hurt him, and I can't believe he would, but I'm afraid it's possible."

Annie gave her a compassionate look. "Jack is your husband?"

"No." The question stung Hannah. "We're—" The words wouldn't come.

"Divorced," Annie said, her voice tender with understanding.

"Yes. I hate the word. I tried everything to keep us together, but he became more and more violent and even dragged a woman home to flaunt at me, then later begged my forgiveness. I couldn't live that way."

Annie gave her a long, searching look. "Do you still love Jack?"

"Love? No. That died with my self-esteem. Jack fought leaving the apartment, but finally he did. He let me be for a while. He didn't even come to see JJ—JJ's short for Jack Junior—but then he started harassing me. Why? I don't know. Maybe he got bored or he's low on funds or couldn't hang on to another woman he could slap around."

"You put up with it a long time?"

Hannah's arms prickled with gooseflesh. "Too long.

He wasn't that way before we married. Occasionally he'd roughhouse, but when I let out a yell, he'd stop. Once we married it was a different story. I was his property, and he figured he could do what he wanted. At first he wasn't too violent—a push, a slap, nasty language—but then, he began to punch and kick me. I realized it would only get worse."

"You're right. It's a sickness. Abuse propagates abuse. He was more than likely an abused child. Sad but true. It doesn't excuse it, but it explains it." Annie lifted her cup and took a sip. "That's not always the case. Some people learn to live normally. They realize it's wrong and not the solution. Others fall into the family-predisposition trap."

"His father was a rough man, but Jack never talked about it much."

"We need to get you a protection order," Annie said.

"What's that?"

"It's a restraining order but for domestic violence cases. I'll give our nurse a call. Mildred Browne is retired, but she comes in as a volunteer and keeps tabs on our guests. We'll take some photos of your face. Then a counselor will talk with you."

Counselor, nurse, photos. The images were too much for Hannah. Tears blurred her vision, and she turned her head away to hide the emotion. She had to remain strong for JJ and for herself. If she didn't, she would crumble and might never get the pieces back together.

Annie's expression grew tender. "It's difficult, I know, but we should document your bruises and cuts. It's the only way we can litigate if necessary."

She touched Hannah's arm where Jack's fingers had left an impression of his violence. "Since your divorce, has this happened before?"

Hannah cringed at the remembrance of her body pinned to the bed, his rough hands pressing against her skin, her nightgown torn in shreds on the floor, the violation of her body.

"Yes, about three weeks ago. I told him I'd call the police if he came again, but when he showed up last night, I realized it wouldn't stop. He'd come back. It would never end." She'd tried to wash away the degradation the night before, but soap and water had only cleaned the surface, not the disgust within her.

Annie rose and headed for the telephone while Hannah sat letting what the woman had said sink in. What good was a protection order? Jack didn't follow the law. He had a law of his own.

As Annie talked on the telephone, Hannah heard the doorbell chime and, instinctively, rose.

"You shouldn't answer the door," Annie said, halting her. "I'll get it."

Hannah had forgotten. She had become a prisoner of sorts, yet sadly, a grateful one.

The bell rang again as Annie ended the call, then hurried into the hallway.

From the kitchen, Hannah heard a man's voice, and she tensed, concerned it might be Jack. Common sense said he couldn't know where to find her. But Jack was shrewd. He would find a way. Hannah eased closer to the kitchen doorway and listened.

"I'm sorry, but you know I can't provide any information like that, Mr. Somerville. It's against our policy."

"I just want to see if she needs anything."

"That's very kind, but we have rules. For now, you'll have to wait."

Hannah's heart tripped, hearing Andrew Somerville's

request. What was his motivation? Compassion? She had been a stranger the night before, and he'd had no idea what she'd gone through, other than seeing her bruises.

The sound of the door closing sent Hannah back to her chair. As she settled into her seat, Annie came through the doorway, a frown pulling at her soft features. "I'm sorry," she said. "Andrew Somerville was inquiring about you, but we can't give out information without your permission. And we need to finish your intake information."

Hannah nodded. "I understand." She'd understood Annie's comment, but she didn't understand Andrew. What did he think he could do for her? "Mr. Somerville found us walking on the road last night. Jack hid my car keys, and after he fell asleep, we had to walk to get away."

Annie's eyebrows arched and lowered within a heartbeat, and Hannah knew Annie wanted an explanation, but Hannah wasn't ready to talk about what happened. "He was drunk and fell asleep," she added, hoping that would suffice.

Annie gave her a nod as if she understood. "I hope you understand about Andrew. If he's a friend—"

"No, I'd never met him before. I don't know why he came here today." Though she knew Andrew meant well, his visit puzzled her.

Despite her questions, gratitude filled her. She and JJ might have had to walk into town if he hadn't come along. He'd taken them into his car despite their appearance and without question. He'd driven them here, he'd offered to carry JJ onto the porch, he'd held an umbrella over her head for shelter. Why couldn't she accept his kindness without questioning it?

While the question still clung to her thoughts, the doorbell rang again, and Hannah's stomach somersaulted. Annie rose to answer, and in moments, Hannah heard a female voice. Her attention was drawn to the kitchen doorway as Annie entered followed by a pleasant-looking woman with graying hair.

"Hi Hannah," she said, extending her hand. "I'm Mildred Browne."

The name took a minute to register as she accepted the handshake. "The nurse?"

Mildred nodded. "Retired, but still a nurse. I've been volunteering at Loving Arms for a few months now." She sat at the table beside Hannah. "Annie told me you've been through a difficult time." Hannah watched the woman's focus shift from her eyes to her bruised cheek, then to her cut lip. "I'd like to take some photos if you don't mind."

"She has bruises on her arms, too," Annie said from behind them.

Hannah felt her back tense. She didn't want to be poked and prodded by these women or by a physician, and she would be if she told Mildred the whole story. Hannah wanted to be free. She wanted her life back.

"Do you have any other marks? Did he harm you in any other way?" Mildred asked.

Hannah swallowed. "These are the only bruises," she said, turning her arms so Mildred could see them and knowing they were the only visible marks of Jack's violence.

"This is difficult, I know," Mildred said. She glanced toward the kitchen doorway. "Perhaps we could find another place to talk?" She glanced at Annie.

"You can use the office," Annie said, gesturing to-

ward the small room on the front of the house adjacent
to the kitchen. "If your son wakes up before you're finished, I'll let you know."

"Thank you," Hannah said, rising and following Mildred into the hallway.

They settled in the office, and Mildred pulled a folder
from her tote, then reached inside and pulled out a camera. The older woman took the snapshots she needed
while Hannah's vision blurred with dots from the flash.

When Mildred finished, she put away the camera,
then opened the folder and drew out a stack of forms.

Hannah recoiled, knowing she had to relive the memory of Jack's violation. She struggled with wanting to
provide all the information, but not wanting to give all
the details. She avoided telling Mildred the worst of
Jack's offenses. What happened had happened, and
she'd get over it.

Her mind slid to Andrew's visit and to the way he'd
offered last night to help her. He'd been insistent and
had made numerous attempts to be kind. Now, as she
thought about it, Andrew's offer triggered a plan.

Hannah hesitated before beginning. "I'd like to get
some of our belongings out of the apartment." She studied Mildred's face, hoping to see empathy.

Mildred nodded. "Certainly. When we're through
here, I can give you a ride to your apartment, if you'd
like. I'm sure Annie will approve."

"I have no family to stay with, and I'm afraid Jack
will be watching the house and then come here to cause
trouble. If we wait a couple of days it might be safer. I
know some people I can ask for help."

"Let's check with Annie," Mildred said. "I'm sure
you'll have no problem as long as the plan is safe."

* * *

On Friday, Andrew stood outside Hannah's apartment complex, still surprised that she had called yesterday and asked for his help. When she explained her scheme, Andrew thought it through and agreed to her idea.

He hit the lock remote on his car, heard the reassuring beep and walked up the sidewalk to the entrance. He eyed the list of occupants: Darwin Lang, Hannah Currey, Carla McCurdy. He pushed the McCurdy button and waited.

"Yes?" a woman's voice said over the intercom.

"I'm Andrew Somerville. I'm here to pick up some boxes."

He heard the click of the intercom followed by a lengthy buzz from the door. Andrew grabbed the knob and turned it. The door opened. He headed up the stairs to find apartment 2D. At the top, he looked down the hallway and saw a woman watching him from a doorway.

"Mr. Somerville?"

"Yes," he said as he headed toward her.

She gave him a smile and beckoned him in. "Hi, I'm Carla. Sorry, but I'm being cautious. This whole thing makes me nervous."

"I understand," Andrew said, stepping into her small apartment. He glanced around the living room, neat but plain and worn. "I know Hannah appreciates what you've done for her."

"No problem. I have her spare key, and she has mine, in case of an emergency." She motioned to a chair. "I'm so glad she's finally taken a stand. Jack'll kill her one day if she doesn't do something now."

Kill her? The words jolted through Andrew's mind.

"You look surprised," Carla said, "but then you don't know him."

Andrew thanked God he didn't know the man capable of this evil. Hannah's and JJ's faces rose in his mind—their looks of fear and pain.

"I was scared to death when I went into the apartment. I thought I heard him leave about three in the morning. He slammed the door so hard it shook the walls, but I was still frightened, worrying maybe he had come back and I hadn't heard him."

The woman's eyes widened, and Andrew sensed her fright. Her words pricked his curiosity. Jack had left at three in the morning. Hannah had left before midnight. If he was her *ex*-husband, why had he stayed so long? If he meant to stop her, why hadn't he followed her?

"When I went in," she continued, "the apartment was empty, except for the note, but then I—"

Andrew held up his hand to halt her. "What note? He left Hannah a note?"

"It's in the box." She gestured to the two boxes near the doorway. "It's vicious. Jack said he'd find her and get even. He said JJ was his and so was she, and he had every right to use her as he wanted."

The sick words rang through Andrew's head, and his thoughts flew, imagining the true danger of the man.

"Jack's a lowlife," Carla said. "Hannah's such a sweet woman, and I can't figure out how they got hooked up. She said he'd changed after they married, but since I've been here, Jack's been nothing but a rat. Hannah says it's because he drinks too much. I suspect drugs."

Drugs? Andrew's pulse gave a swift kick.

"But I have to admit," Carla said, "he's never hurt JJ. Still I was relieved when she made him move out, but that hasn't stopped him. He's sick."

Andrew stepped back, startled by the words that flew from her mouth. But could she be correct? Had Jack gotten hooked on drugs?

Apparently noticing the look on Andrew's face, Carla's eyes widened, and she blinked. "I'm so sorry to rattle on like this. You're a stranger, and I must sound horrible. I'm not a judgmental person normally, but when I watch a woman—"

"Please," Andrew said, lifting his hand to calm her, "I'm not judging you. I'm just surprised. I don't really know Hannah. I picked her and her son up along the road the night she left."

"That poor boy," Carla said, shaking her head, her features filling with sadness. "He's never had a father. Jack's only around when he has nowhere else to go, and then he's a madman. I'm surprised JJ is the sweet boy that he is."

Hearing the woman's words, Andrew's gut ached, wondering about the child's future. And Hannah's.

"Hannah."

Hannah looked up when she heard Annie calling outside her bedroom. A tap-tap followed. She rose and pulled open the door. "Hi."

"You have company."

Company? Her pulse skipped as possibilities flew through her mind: police, detective, social worker, nurse? "Who's here to see me?"

"Andrew Somerville." She motioned toward the living room. "He has the things from your apartment."

"But I thought—"

"Rules are made to be broken." Annie grinned. "He's been so helpful, and it's not like he's a stranger. Now that your paperwork is filled out and you've settled in, I see no reason for you not to have a visitor."

Hannah felt heat roll up her chest. "Thanks. I'll be right there."

Annie nodded and walked away while Hannah darted to the small mirror hanging in her room to check her hair. She looked at her lips to see if they still had color. Lipstick was the only makeup she'd carried in her purse the night she arrived. She found her comb and dragged it through the tangles, uncomfortable with the strange feelings that now assailed her. Her pulse had skipped when Annie said Andrew's name, and she barely knew the man. She dropped the comb onto the dresser and drew in a lengthy breath to settle her nerves, then headed to the living room.

Andrew stood near the door with two large cartons at his feet. "Hi," he said as she came through the doorway.

She felt a flush rise up her neck. She'd forgotten how good-looking he was. "Hi," she said. They'd only spoken on the telephone since he'd dropped her off the few nights before, and now in the light she admired his strong jaw and well-shaped mouth, curved into a smile.

The warm look grabbed her heart and gave it a squeeze. She raised her hand as if to fend away the sensation that confused her. She gestured toward the boxes. "Thanks. I'm anxious to get into my own clothes."

"You're welcome." He glanced beyond her. "Where's JJ?"

"He's in the backyard, playing. He misses his friends already."

"I bet."

Hannah shifted feet, feeling awkward and not sure what was protocol at Loving Arms. He remained standing, and so did she. Hoping to catch Annie's eye, Hannah glanced toward the office, but she wasn't there.

"Would you like to sit?" she asked, wanting to dispel the tense feeling she had.

Andrew gazed at the chairs and sofa without answering. Finally he shifted to the nearest chair and sat. "I hope I brought everything you need."

Hannah followed his action and sank onto the sofa. "I'm sure Carla found all the things I mentioned." The conversation continued to seem strained and unreal.

"Speaking of Carla..." He looked uneasy as he glanced toward the boxes. "...she found a note in the apartment."

"A note?" Hannah's pulse quickened again.

"It's in the top carton." He swung his arm toward the box.

Hannah rose, strode to the box and unfolded the lid. On the top, she saw Jack's scribble, and she eyed his message. The words stabbed at her, leaving her with a dire hopeless feeling.

She turned to Andrew. "Did you read it?"

"No, but Carla gave me the gist." He dropped his gaze to the floor. "I'm sorry, Hannah. You shouldn't have to go through this. No one should."

His sincerity washed over her. What could she say? She folded the note into a little square, wanting to flush it down the toilet. "I can't let him get away with this."

"Call the police. That's your only option."

Her only option. Her mind swirled with frustration, knowing Andrew had stated the truth.

* * *

Andrew stood outside Philip and Jemma's door and rang the bell. Hannah had permeated his thoughts all afternoon. He'd enjoyed visiting with her earlier in the day. She'd been uneasy at first, but then he had, too.

Hannah seemed a devoted mother—gentle and loving—and despite the bruises and bloodied lip, she was very pretty. She didn't deserve to spend her life running from problems. Problems. His past had been filled with them. Was that why Hannah had lingered in his thoughts?

A sound from inside caught Andrew's attention, and when Philip opened the door, an appetizing aroma drifted out to meet him. "Something smells good," he said, stepping over the threshold.

"Let me take your jacket," Philip said.

Andrew slipped it off, and as soon as his foot hit the carpet, Ellie's voice pierced the air. "Unkie And'woo."

Andrew grinned at her garbled greeting. She opened her arms wide, and he handed Philip his offering of a bouquet of fresh flowers. "Hi, sugar cakes," he said scooping her into the air as she giggled and kicked her feet.

"Hi, Andrew," Jemma said, coming through the doorway.

Andrew set Ellie back on the carpet and retrieved the flowers from Philip. "A thank-you for the meal. It smells delicious."

"It's the best I could do. Getting close to the oven is dangerous." She patted her rounded belly and sent him a smile. "It won't be long now."

"I'm sure you're both excited." He glanced at Philip and witnessed the purest love on his brother's face. "Did you give in and find out yet? Boy or girl?"

Jemma shrugged. "No, we are still doing it the old fashioned way." She took a few steps forward and curled her arm around Philip's waist. "We're letting the Lord surprise us."

As she held the bouquet of flowers and stood beside Philip, Andrew imagined her as a bride. His stomach tightened, knowing that he'd missed their wedding.

Philip gave her a quick kiss, and she grinned, lifting the flowers into the air as a salute. "These are beautiful but they need water, and the two of you need dinner."

Seeing their happiness drove Andrew's sorrow home even deeper, and he didn't want to face his feelings. A widower, Philip had been childless until he married Jemma. Andrew knew his brother well enough to know his workaholic schedule in the past hadn't afforded him time to plan a family or even want one. But now, getting to know Jemma and seeing her warm smile and youthful vigor, Andrew could understand how she had broken through Philip's barricade. He'd finally become a father at fifty-one.

Ellie tugged at Andrew's pantleg, and he crouched to give her the attention she wanted. She was a miniature of Jemma, blond with delicate features, but her coaxing blue eyes were like Philip's.

Andrew played with Ellie until Jemma called them to dinner. He enjoyed the meal of Swiss steak, and while she put Ellie to bed, he and Philip returned to the living room.

"Is something bothering you?" Philip asked. "You seem tense. I noticed when we talked a couple days ago at the resort."

Philip's question struck Andrew between the eyes.

He'd tried to cover his preoccupation, but he guessed he hadn't done a very good job. "It's just life. Nothing you can do anything about."

"I'm your brother, Andrew. If you're having a problem, then I'd like to help."

"Some problems are internal. No help available."

Philip shook his head. "You're a Christian, brother. We both know that God can lift us from our troubles. He is our help and shield. We just have to call on Him."

"I've called on Him enough." Andrew squirmed, knowing that Philip wouldn't stop unless Jemma came into the room. "It's me. Really. I've messed up my life. You know that. I'm nine years younger than you with a life ahead of me, yet I see it passing me by."

Philip frowned. "Why? You can have what you want if you put your mind to it."

"Maybe that's the problem. I don't believe I can. I've limited my ability to earn a solid income." Andrew lifted his hand to stop Philip from responding. "I know you gave me a job when I got back home, and I appreciate it, but I wasted my inheritance. All of this would have been half mine if I'd had the common sense to follow in your path—the path Dad laid out for us. Instead I was resentful. I could never compete with your ability, and I probably feel the same today."

"I'm retired. No competition anymore, and I'm sorry you feel that way. I shared Dad's vision. I can't deny that, and he knew what he was doing."

"He did, and I don't resent that at all."

"But that doesn't limit your ability."

"Philip, I look at you with a wife like Jemma, a sweet little daughter like Ellie and a new baby on the way, and then I look at me. What do I have? Worldly experiences, nothing I can brag about and nothing that I even want to remember."

"You're still young, Andrew. You can have a wife and children."

"But I don't have the financial security. I have nothing to offer a family."

"That's not all a family needs. You have the capacity for loving and protecting. You're great with kids. Look at you with Ellie. You've come home, giving of yourself. You're capable and intelligent."

The vision of JJ in his sodden pajamas flashed through Andrew's mind, and he released a ragged sigh. "Intelligent? I'm not so sure about that." Philip had been correct about his ability to love and protect. He did feel those emotions for Ellie and, to his surprise, Hannah and JJ. Even though he barely knew them, the two of them had rattled his senses. They were feelings that confused him.

"You were young when you left. You weren't looking at life with wisdom but with the spirit of adventure. Who's to say that you couldn't succeed now? And don't forget you have the trust fund."

Irritation bristled through Andrew. "I can't take that money. I told you before."

"It's yours. Dad left it for you."

But why? Andrew knew he had neither earned it, nor deserved it. "The money is yours, Philip."

Philip shook his head but didn't say any more.

Before the conversation went further, Jemma reappeared in the doorway. "I'm making some fresh coffee." Her face looked flushed.

"You're tired," Andrew said.

"No, I love having you here. I'm just weary from lugging around this extra weight." She grinned as she lowered herself into a chair, and Andrew smiled back.

Seeing the three of them—Philip, Jemma and Ellie—triggered Andrew's thoughts. Family was so important and so powerful, but what about people like Hannah? She had struggled so much; she seemed to be a good person. Carla's comments about Hannah echoed in his mind.

"You're quiet," Jemma said.

Andrew jerked his head upward, realizing he'd drifted off in thought. "I had a strange experience earlier this week and then today. I can't seem to get it off my mind."

"Strange?" Philip asked, curiosity and concern written on his face.

"On Wednesday I was coming back from Grand Rapids about midnight, and I saw someone walking along the road." He told them about the incident while Philip and Jemma both nodded, their gazes intent.

"Oh my," Jemma said, compassion filling her face. "The poor family. I just can't imagine."

"We take things for granted," Philip said.

Andrew knew that's where they differed. He didn't take things for granted any longer. He regretted what he'd done and hoped God had forgiven him. But Andrew hadn't been as forgiving of himself as the Lord. He'd been trying to repent for his waste and the neglect of his family. Yet how could he?

"We'll keep them in our prayers," Jemma said.

Andrew told them about retrieving Hannah's belongings earlier that day, but he didn't mention the excitement he'd felt talking with Hannah—a feeling he didn't yet understand.

"Speaking of Loving Arms," Philip said. "Bill from the volunteer committee told me Annie DeWitt phoned about a maintenance problem they're having. I'm guessing it's ants. She spotted sawdust on the porch floor. We need to get someone over there to check it out. Bill's been tied up with some family issues, and—"

"I'll talk with him on Sunday and take care of it." Andrew knew he had an ulterior motive for going to the shelter. His interest extended beyond the bounds of charity, yet the more he thought about it, the more excitement and dread he felt. Would his involvement only lead to trouble?

Chapter Three

Hannah tried to relax as she stood outside Loving Hair Salon the next day. She wondered how much she should tell her co-workers. Yet Hannah realized she had to be honest. A counselor she'd spoken to had stressed the necessity of a safe work environment. Annie had even arranged a ride to and from work for her as a safety precaution.

When she stepped inside, Macy looked up and gave her a wave. "Feeling better?"

"A little," she said, hoping her makeup covered the bruise. She slipped off her coat and hurried past the beautician toward the storage room where she placed her belongings, then gathered a stack of towels and capes to stock the front.

Her nerves jangled. If even one customer noticed her face, she'd be the new topic of conversation for the day. Sometimes they forgot that beneath the drone of the hair dryers their gossip could be heard by everyone.

Hannah went about stocking the work stations, keeping the right side of her face away from Macy until she found the courage to talk with her. Her thoughts drifted to Andrew's visit the day before. He confused her with his kindness.

Before she could finish, the bell on the door gave a ding, and their first customer arrived. Saturday meant a busy day, and between the phone calls and new customers, Hannah was surprised that two hours had gone by when she looked up to see Andrew coming through the entrance.

As she towel-dried a woman's hair, he watched her from a chair in the waiting area. She tilted her head in a subtle hello, then sent the customer to her stylist and turned to wipe her hands. When she swung around, Andrew stood beside her. Hannah glanced at Macy and noticed the questioning look on her face.

"Did you want your hair washed?" Macy asked, as if wondering why he'd walked into the work area.

He halted and did a double take. "If that's okay?"

"Sure," Macy said before refocusing on her client.

Hannah held her breath, wondering what Andrew wanted.

"I remembered you said you worked here," Andrew said, talking in a near whisper as she steered him toward the sink.

Hannah eyed him, not knowing what to say. She motioned for him to be seated, then wrapped a towel around his neck and draped a plastic cape around him. She eased the chair back, and he reclined against the basin. "You didn't really want a shampoo, did you?" She heard his nervous chuckle.

"Not really, but I do need a haircut." He stopped and arched his head upward, looking toward Macy. "I didn't want to cause any trouble by walking back here. I just wondered how you're doing." His eyes shifted to her cheek, then her lip. "The bruise already looks better."

Unbidden, her hand lifted and touched her swollen cheek. "I covered it with makeup. Thanks." She checked the water temperature, wet his hair, then pumped the shampoo bottle and filled her palm.

"How's JJ? Is he missing home?"

"He's adjusting. It's as good as can be expected." Hannah lathered his head, running her fingers through his short thick hair. For the first time, her attention drew to the silver patches streaking his dark hair. His youthful face belied the gray. She plied her fingertips into his scalp, finding the closeness distracting while trying to control the question that kept nagging at her. Lifting her sudsy hands, she paused. "I don't really understand why you're so concerned about us."

Andrew's eyes flew open as if startled by her query. He appeared to gain composure, and deep dimples flickered at the corners of his mouth. "I've asked myself the same question."

The look on his face made Hannah grin back, yet she was still uncertain about his motivation. His spicy scent mingled with the fragrance of the shampoo.

After a lengthy silence, Andrew turned his head toward her, and his expression changed as if something pressed on his mind, but he remained quiet. She rinsed, then shampooed again, then added conditioner with the final rinse before having him sit up.

Once he'd straightened, he looked her in the eyes. "What about the note? Did you call the police?"

His question startled her. "Yes."

"Has your husband written you notes like this before?" Hannah's back stiffened. "He's my *ex*-husband. I told you." She grabbed a towel and dropped it over his hair. "And that question is rather personal."

"I'm sorry, but I can't understand how any man can treat a woman so—"

Hannah tousled his hair with the towel to dry it with more vengeance than she meant, then pulled the towel from his head. "The shelter's helping me handle things. I'm grateful for all you've done, and I appreciate your concern, but—" She tilted her head toward Macy and a customer. "I haven't spoken to my boss yet."

"I understand." He rose from the chair and slipped a tip into her hands. "I'm sorry. I didn't mean to pry."

Hannah struggled with the uncomfortable situation. Macy called him to her station, giving Hannah a reprieve. She watched him be seated, then went back to her work.

Andrew cringed as he settled into the chair. Why had he been so blatant? He could have said hello and let it go at that. Anything but what he'd done. He couldn't blame her for her irritation. She didn't know him or his intentions any better than she knew the TV anchorman delivering the news or the mailman bringing the mail. For that matter, he didn't know his intentions, either.

Andrew answered the stylist's question about the type of cut he wanted and tried to avoid staring at Hannah. Since Carla had mentioned drugs, he'd been more than on edge. People hooked on drugs changed, and another thing Carla had told him lingered in his mind. She'd said Hannah had left the apartment after Jack had fallen asleep. He'd tried to make sense out of the statement, but he'd left it alone. Maybe he didn't want to know the answer. He figured a woman should feel safe in her home, but Hannah couldn't with a man like Jack.

Home. The word unsettled him at times. In Detroit, he'd met many young women who'd gotten involved with shady men who'd used them for their own purpose—from drugs to prostitution. They'd been young and innocent, leaving home to make their way in the world as he had done, but they didn't have the financial backing he'd had, and they had been too proud to return to their families. He could relate to that in a heartbeat.

He'd never had to cheat or use people, but Andrew had found himself eating one meal a day and trying to shine his worn shoes while he hoped to make at least one business deal that would succeed. Why hadn't he realized he was intelligent but just didn't have the same vision for creating a business that Philip and his father had?

Sitting in front of the salon mirror, Andrew sidled a look at Hannah shampooing a customer's hair. His mind flooded with the feeling of her fingers against his scalp, the scent of shampoo and the earlier sweet fragrance when he'd walked over to her.

The stylist snipped his hair, buzzed the trimmer along his neckline, then brushed away the cuttings. When she finished, he rose, forcing himself not to look Hannah's way. After Andrew left a tip, Macy called another customer as he headed for the reception desk. To his surprise, Hannah stepped behind the register. She rang up the fee for a wash and haircut, and, at a loss for words, he dug into his wallet and handed her the bills.

When she gave him the change, Hannah sent him an apologetic smile. The look released the pressure in his chest, and he smiled back.

Instead of saying goodbye, Hannah followed him to the doorway. "I'm sorry I was so touchy today," she said. "I appreciate all you've done."

"I didn't mean to upset you," Andrew said. "Asking personal questions wasn't proper. I'm sorry."

She looked as if she had something to say, but she didn't.

"You and your son have been on my mind, because I—" Andrew stopped himself. Apparently Hannah didn't know his pitiful story. Right now, he wanted to leave it that way.

She appeared to wait for him to finish his sentence.

"Take care, and don't rush back to your apartment. I'm sure you're safer where you are."

"Thanks, but I can't stay there forever."

"You need to change your apartment locks."

She nodded. "I have lots to do before I go home."

"Take care," he said again, pulling open the door. The words had slipped from his mouth without a thought. *Take care.* The words meant nothing to a woman fearing for her life.

He saw Hannah's wave through the glass and suddenly felt like a kid who'd won the brass ring on the carousel.

Once in his car, Andrew checked his watch. He turned the key in the ignition and pulled away, once again feeling empty and unsettled. When he'd left home years ago, he'd wanted success, money and power. What Hannah wanted was security and independence.

Andrew thought back to his affluent home with stable parents and a Christian upbringing. He'd been given many luxuries as a child. Not until he'd left to make his fortune did he realize how hard his father had worked and how intelligent he'd been. Today, Andrew's deepest regret was not returning home for his father's funeral. Being down and out, he couldn't face the town nor his brother. Admitting the truth had been too hard then.

He thought about how Hannah had struggled to acknowledge her failed marriage. Violence destroyed families. It destroyed lives. He'd seen it in Detroit when he'd ventured there, and in Chicago where he'd tried his hand at another failed business. He'd never been a violent man, but he'd seen it. It killed the spirit and left families fearful and hopeless.

He wanted to know more about domestic violence. What could Hannah do to improve her son's life and her own? He felt driven to find the answer, and he turned the steering wheel and nosed his sedan into the Loving Public Library parking lot.

He climbed the few steps into the building and observed the long racks of books. Ian Barry's wife, Esther, smiled at him from the front desk, and Andrew headed her way.

"Hi," she said, "what brings you here?" She chuckled at her question. "Books, I suppose."

"Research. I want to read up on domestic violence."

She didn't ask but led him into the Dewey Decimal 300s. "Here they are. 362.829. Family and domestic violence." She pointed to numerous books on the subject. "You'll find a lot of helpful information on the Internet or our database, too."

"Thanks, Esther," he said, already eyeing the books that looked most promising. Andrew slipped a couple from the shelves, wandered to a nearby table and sat.

He opened a cover and flipped to the introduction. Facts immediately jumped out at him, facts he wanted to brush away and eliminate. Nearly one-third of American women were abused by husbands or live-in partners. Violence by an intimate partner accounted for over one-fifth of all violent crimes against women.

Andrew's stomach churned as he read from an FBI crime report. Among all female murder victims in the U.S., one-third were slain by husbands or boyfriends. He fell back against the chair. *Murder?* Could this happen to Hannah? And JJ? Had her neighbor been correct? Andrew's gaze slipped to a magazine statistic. Child abuse occurred in thirty to sixty percent of family abuse cases.

The facts and statistics pressed on his heart, but he felt God's hand leading him along this path. He'd learned much from his life choices, yet what could he do for this woman and child? Nothing really. Hannah was in control of her own life. He could do nothing but pray.

Amazed at his urgent compulsion to help, Andrew rose and checked out the books. Outside he took a deep breath of fresh air and tucked the volumes under his arm. He wanted to clear the dark feelings from his mind. He longed to figure out what God wanted him to do.

A week later, Hannah sat on the back porch of Loving Arms. Though a chilly Monday morning, the sun felt good, and she was tired of feeling trapped indoors. She'd called the apartment manager to request her locks be changed, and when that was completed, she longed to go home.

Annie had encouraged her to give Jack's note to the police the week before, and Hannah had been granted a protection order. She hoped that Jack would get a lengthy jail sentence for his threats and give her time to move or make changes in her life. But would it be enough, and would it stop Jack from another attack after he was released? Her questions were endless.

She loved having the day off. She'd worked long hours Saturday and Sunday so today felt like a gift. Her gaze shifted to the backyard where JJ played on a rusty set of swings. If she had the money, Hannah thought, she'd buy a new set of playground equipment for the shelter.

In the week and a half she'd been there, a few women had arrived, but most spent a day or two and then left to stay with family. Hannah rarely missed her family— her family had created their own realm of problems— but at times like this, having someone to turn to would have made life easier.

Instead she felt grateful that Loving Arms had given them a home for the time being. So far, Jack hadn't bothered her here, and she was grateful for that. Soon she would start a new job at a chocolate shop, and she'd feel safer, but going back home still concerned her.

Conversation from inside interrupted Hannah's thoughts, and she glanced over her shoulder to hear who'd arrived. She could make out Annie's voice, then a man's deep chuckle, followed by Annie's laugh.

When the screen door squeaked, Hannah pivoted her head to see who Annie was bringing outside. When she saw Andrew's face, her pulse skipped.

"How are you doing?" he asked, seeming pleased to see her.

Hannah nodded.

"I'm fine, thanks, and you?" The polite conversation seemed silly, and she recognized the same realization in his eyes.

"What brings you here?" Hannah asked, giving in to her curiosity.

"Andrew's part of a volunteer group from United Christian Church. They do repairs and maintenance on the building," Annie said, answering for him. "We're so grateful for their help."

"I'm happy to help." Andrew shifted his gaze to the porch ceiling. "So this is where you spotted the sawdust?"

Annie led him to the edge of the porch. "Right here." She pointed down, then up to the ceiling. "I think it came from up there."

He tilted his head and eyed the support beam, then gave it a poke. A shower of fine beige dust fell to the floor. "You're right. That's your problem."

"I suppose the roof will fall in if we don't get that fixed," Annie said, giving him a crooked smile.

"Could happen. It looks like carpenter ants. They love damp wood." Andrew dragged a chair to the spot and raised himself to get a closer look.

The phone's ring chimed from inside, and Annie grasped the door handle. "You can tell me what needs to be done when you finish." She opened the door and hurried to answer.

Andrew stepped down from the chair and scooted it back against the wall. He made some notations on a pad, then stepped into the yard and focused on the porch roof, then the flooring. When he finished, he sat on the top step and leaned against the porch column, his body turned to face her.

"I'm glad to see you're still here," he said, flipping closed the notepad and tucking it into his jacket pocket.

"I'm not. It's hard on JJ. And me."

"But you're safe." Andrew's eyes grew distant, and he turned, gazing at her son playing in the yard. "You can't take chances."

"I know," Hannah said. She hadn't wanted to take

chances and that's why she'd divorced Jack. Her gaze shifted to Andrew's handsome profile, wondering if he truly understood. He'd never known a difficult life, she guessed, so why try to explain it all to him?

Andrew rose and brushed dirt from his jeans, then wandered into the yard. She watched him amble toward JJ and crouch to talk to him. Their voices didn't reach her, but JJ nodded and chattered with him like an old friend.

Andrew tousled JJ's hair, and when the child showed him a ball, Andrew moved back and pitched a few to him. His gentle way touched Hannah's heart, yet surprised her.

JJ had never connected with a man in his life. Jack wasn't around and hadn't given him much attention, except when JJ whined. Then Jack's voice raised the hair on her arms and caused JJ to cry. If Jack had lifted a hand, Hannah would have divorced him sooner.

Divorce. The word pelted her with guilt. Despite her spiritual lapse, her mother had raised her to believe marriage was for better or worse, and she'd planned to make it work. But Jack had sickened her when he flaunted his adultery in her face. That day she'd made her decision. God did not expect her to accept Jack's abuse and adultery.

Andrew's focus drifted to Hannah. Though their conversation today had seemed stilted, she continued to intrigue him, but he forced his focus back to JJ. The boy had missed the ball again but scurried after it to try one more time. The child had determination, just like his mother.

While JJ scampered to retrieve the ball, Andrew's sympathy arose, thinking of the life the child had lived and things he'd probably heard and seen. He recalled the statistics in the book he'd borrowed from the library. The facts sickened him, and he'd had to control himself from spitting out the horrifying figures to Hannah as they had talked.

One sentence rang in his mind—children from violent homes engage in more risk-taking behavior and may become violent adults. The thought wrenched his heart. Children were the innocent victims of family problems.

"Keep practicing," Andrew said, as he gave the ball a final toss before heading back to the porch. He saw Hannah's smile and felt a grin grow on his face. "He's trying. He'll get it."

"He's had no one to teach him."

Her comment drew his attention to the fading bruise on her cheek, then to her mouth. The cut had disappeared and in its place, Andrew now admired her well-shaped mouth and upturned lips. His pulse heightened until he pulled away his gaze.

"What are you going to do?" Andrew asked, lowering himself to the top step and leaning against the support.

"Change my door locks. Take a new job. Be more careful. I don't know what else."

He sat closer to her this time, and her sweet floral scent permeated the air. He savored the fragrance before speaking again. "How about police protection?"

"I was granted a protection order, but I'm afraid it won't stop Jack. He's so vicious he…" She paused and looked away.

Andrew didn't know if he should speak or wait.

"I'm sorry," she said. "Let's forget my problems."

He wanted to remind her that God promised to bear her burdens, but he recalled that when he was in her shoes, he didn't remember that, either. If he had remembered, he'd been too ashamed to ask the Lord for help.

She gave a faint shrug, then waved to JJ who was tossing the ball in the air and trying to catch it.

"He misses his friends," Hannah said. "I'm thinking we can go back once the locks are changed. At least I'll have the protection order, and I can always hope it helps. Maybe with the note he left, the judge will give Jack some jail time."

Andrew's next question seemed almost pointless, thinking of Jack's compulsive behavior. "Have you pressed charges?"

"Yes." Her gaze drifted from him to JJ.

"If you need someone to help with anything, just ask. I'd be happy to do what I can."

"Thanks," she said. "You've already done too much."

He didn't respond, his thoughts captured by a new question. "Do you feel safe at work?"

"I don't know, but as I said, I start a new job in mid-May. Jack won't know where I am unless he follows me." Her downcast eyes snapped upward suddenly and her gaze captured his. "Although that's not beyond him."

Andrew agreed. He wondered what was keeping the guy from finding her now. "Where's the new job?"

"Loving Chocolate. I'll be a candymaker there."

"Candymaker. Sounds like a sweet place to work." He grimaced at his silly comment, but she smiled and that pleased him. He'd begun to notice that many things pleased him about Hannah.

Before their conversation continued, a commotion sounded from inside, and his gut knotted. Hannah rose, but Andrew's arm flew forward to stop her. "Stay here," he said before he darted inside.

He met Annie in the hallway and, seeing her ashen face, skidded to a stop. "What is it? What's all the noise?"

Annie pressed her hand against her chest. "He's after Hannah, and he's determined to get in."

Chapter Four

Andrew motioned Annie toward the shelter's office. "Call 911," Andrew whispered, "while I get Hannah and JJ inside before Jack tries the back door." He was certain the violent intruder was Hannah's ex-husband. "I'll talk with him."

Annie faltered. "No. It's not your responsibility. I can't—"

"You can," he said, again steering her toward the phone. Relieved when she followed his instructions, Andrew dashed to the back door.

Hannah had already come through the doorway, clutching JJ to her side. "What is it?" Panic filled her eyes as if she already knew the answer.

Jack's rantings resounded through the front entrance, and JJ began to cry as he clasped his mother's leg.

"You'll be fine, son," Andrew said, closing and locking the back door. He motioned toward the hallway. "Get into your room and pull the window shades. I'll take care of it."

Hannah did as he asked, and as Andrew raced past

the office doorway, Annie's tense voice met his ears. His teeth ground together, his jaw aching with tension. Witnessing the fear in Hannah's eyes and seeing the boy's fright, too, fired him into action. Andrew had never been a fighter, but now his dark past rose up to meet him, for once, without guilt. He'd learned to be strong and maneuver well in difficult situations. Today that skill could be his ally.

He grasped the doorknob and jerked open the door, not knowing what might happen but asking God to be his fortress.

The action appeared to startle Jack, and he stumbled backward for a moment before regaining control.

The stench of alcohol attacked Andrew's senses. Jack's unshaven face sagged while his bloodshot eyes narrowed. "Who are you?" he barked.

"Who are you?" Andrew asked, knowing full well who he was.

"You don't belong here. This is a women's center."

"Then you don't belong here either," Andrew responded, struggling to keep his voice calm.

Jack's courage rose, and he drew himself to full height and took a step forward, his breath reeking in Andrew's face. "You're hiding my family in there. I've waited more than a week for her to go home. Hannah's my wife. She belongs to me."

She belongs to me. The words disgusted Andrew. A wife should be cherished and protected. A man *owned* a car or a boat, not a wife. Andrew longed to tell that to Jack, but he knew it would be useless.

"Nothing in this house belongs to you," Andrew said. His pulse jarred, hearing a police siren sound in the distance.

Jack flinched at his comment. His fists balled into tight knots, and he lifted one, then shook it threateningly in Andrew's face.

Andrew held his ground while his reflexes jerked in readiness and stated flatly, "You'd be smart to leave calmly. You made a mistake coming here."

"It's no mistake," Jack said, drawing back his fist.

In a flash, Andrew captured Jack's arm and forced him back.

Jack's strength buckled, and he faltered as the siren drew closer. He wrenched his arm from Andrew's strong grasp and glanced over his shoulder. "You haven't heard the last of me." Jack jerked away, cursing, and darted toward his car, but before he reached it, a squad car skidded to a halt, and two officers raced toward him.

Jack kicked at one officer and made another move for his car door, but the second officer bounded around the trunk and slammed him against the car frame. Jack let out a string of filthy language before the officers pulled him from the door and cuffed him.

Andrew watched while they put him into the police car, figuring Jack had increased the charges against him by resisting arrest. While an officer moved Jack's vehicle from the driveway, the other stepped onto the porch. "We'll need someone to come down to the station and make a statement. I'll send a wrecker over for the car."

"I'll drive her down," Andrew said. He watched the officer stride from the porch, realizing that his life was now entangled in Hannah's, and he needed the mess like he needed an ulcer.

Hannah sat in silence, listening to the hum of the car engine. She'd filed another report against Jack, and now she wondered what would happen next. She glanced at Andrew's profile, his jaw set, his hands gripping the steering wheel, looking as determined as she usually felt. But today was an exception. After Jack's appearance at the shelter that morning, her life seemed fragile, her confidence shaken. She had no answers for her problems any more than Andrew had.

Eyeing him for a moment, Hannah noticed Andrew's lips move as if ready to speak, but instead, he pressed them together, keeping his focus on the highway. His strong profile offered Hannah a sense of safety. His classic nose, his well-defined chin, his jaw darkened by a faint five-o'clock shadow captured her awareness, and she struggled to avert her gaze to the passenger window. She didn't want him to notice she'd been gawking at him.

The awareness troubled her. Her interest in men had vanished after her horrifying marriage and divorce. She feared falling in love again, feared trusting a man to be the same person after the wedding as he was before. Jack had made a one-hundred-and-eighty-degree turn. How could she ever have confidence to trust again?

Yet despite her misgivings, Andrew lingered in her thoughts. His kindness, his concern and Christian love seemed to wind around her heart and give it a little tug each time he appeared. At this moment, her pulse had kicked up a notch just because she was beside him in the car.

"I think it's more than changing locks," Andrew said, breaking the silence and her thoughts.

"More than changing locks?" She studied his face, this time feeling free to venture a direct look. His comment had come out of nowhere.

"You won't be safe in that apartment. Even new locks won't keep him out."

"You mean Jack," she said, assured that's who he meant.

He glanced her way as if surprised at her statement. "Yes, Jack. The officer said the proceeding will probably be in about ten days so I'm hoping they'll hold him in jail until then, and—"

"They have to put him behind bars now."

"Jack's a man who doesn't follow rules. You said it yourself. If he does get jail time, I'm afraid he'll just come back once he's released." Andrew's knuckles turned white as his grip on the wheel tightened.

"So what can I do?"

"Move."

Move. Yes, she'd thought of that. She planned it, but right now she didn't have the energy or time to think about anything. "I want to get out of Loving Arms. I need to get home."

"Soon you'll have the perfect time to move, Hannah. Jack resisted arrest, too, so I'm sure he'll get some jail time. I'll help you find a place." He slid his hand in his pocket, pulled out a cell phone and shoved it toward her. "Call Annie or whoever's on staff and see if they'll keep an eye on JJ for a little longer."

Hannah took the phone from him and grasped it in her lap. "But I can't—"

"We'll pick up a newspaper and check out what's available. I'll look at the apartments and narrow them down to the best two or three. It'll save you time."

Hannah's mind rebelled against his words. She didn't want to be pushed into something before she was ready, and what business was it of his? She opened her mouth to tell him that but closed it again, realizing he had her best interest at heart, and he was probably right. If she had a new job and a new apartment, Jack would have a harder time finding her once he was free again.

Uncertain, she picked up the cell phone and looked at it. Andrew had turned on the power switch already so she pressed in the numbers and hit Call. Annie answered and her response was what Hannah expected.

"No problem at all," Annie said. "JJ and my daughter Gracelynne are playing together. To be honest, he's keeping an eye on her for me."

"Thanks so much. I won't be too much longer," Hannah said before she clicked off.

In a moment, Andrew had pulled into a coffee shop parking lot. He hurried around to Hannah's door before she could put her foot on the ground. Until she'd met Andrew, no man had helped her from a car in years.

She walked beside him, still puzzled at his interest in her and JJ, yet touched by his concern. She'd felt at home in her apartment with Carla close beside her. Now, if she moved, she'd have to adjust to new neighbors, a new home, and a new job—too many things for her at this point in time.

Andrew paused to drop coins into the newspaper box outside the restaurant. He tucked a paper under his arm and opened the door for her.

Hannah stepped inside and was barraged by the scent of French fries and burgers. She hadn't eaten since her simple breakfast, and her stomach rumbled, reminding her.

Andrew gestured to a booth, and she slid in staying on the outer edge. Without seeming to notice or care, Andrew sat across from her and placed the newspaper on the tabletop. He slid two menus from behind the metal napkin holder and handed her one. "I'm hungry. How about you?" He glanced at his watch.

She gave a faint nod.

"Good. Let's have lunch."

Though disconcerted, she perused the menu and settled on an unhealthy burger, but instead of fries, she ordered a salad with fat-free dressing. The discrepancy reflected her life—a crazy blend of good and bad, order and disorder, positive and negative.

Today seemed no different. Though Andrew had given so much of himself in generosity, Hannah sensed he hid something behind his quiet demeanor. He talked about her but said so little about himself. She'd pondered it before. Perhaps his family's wealth kept him from flaunting his superior lifestyle. Maybe his faith controlled his ego.

When the waitress returned with their coffee and glasses of water, Andrew unrolled the newspaper and flipped through the pages until he found the want ads. "Here," he said, sliding half the paper to her. "There's some on this page and some there." His index finger pressed against the column.

Hannah shifted the paper in front of her, fascinated that Andrew's hands were rougher-looking than she'd expected—no manicure. They were hands that looked strong, as if they'd worked somewhere besides a white-collar job.

"Have you always worked in the Somerville business?" she asked, surprised she'd spoken so boldly.

His jaw twitched, and Hannah feared she'd overstepped her boundaries. His gaze caught hers with a guarded look of surprise. "No. I did my own thing for a while."

"Oh," she said, cautioning herself not to continue, but his reaction puzzled her. She could ask Annie about him, but the Bible heeded believers against gossip, and though she felt abandoned by God at times, she still followed the Commandments.

Instead, Hannah studied the want ads, wondering if changed locks might not solve the problem. If Jack couldn't get in, it would give her time to call the police again.

"Here's a two-bedroom apartment, and the price looks good." Andrew turned the newspaper so she could read the description.

"I can't afford that," she said, ashamed that she had to admit that to a man who'd never known poverty.

He nodded without reaction and pulled the newspaper back toward himself again.

Hannah's throat tightened. She didn't want to admit her finances to anyone. The desperateness of her situation rolled over her. Why would she let Jack chase her away from her home? Her apartment met her need within her budget. She wasn't going to let Jack or a man she barely knew manipulate her to move. She drew up her shoulders and faced him. "Andrew, I've decided—"

"Burger?"

Hannah faltered and looked up. The waitress stood above her with the order. "The burger's mine," she said, irritated by the woman's timing.

With his order in front of him, Andrew unwrapped the napkin from around his silverware and placed it on the table. "Do you mind if I pray?"

"Pray?" She faltered, then realized he wanted to bless the food. Instead of responding, Hannah bowed her head.

"Lord, we don't understand your purpose. We don't always know why we face trials, but we know You are with us through it all. Father, we thank you for every blessing, for this food and this day. We ask You to place Your loving hand on our lives and protect us from evil. Amen."

"Amen" fell from Hannah's lips while the prayer washed over her. What trials had Andrew faced? Was he placating her and her needs? The more she thought, the more puzzled she became.

Hannah lifted her fork and speared a lettuce leaf. Her appetite had shrunk with her thoughts. She'd opened her mouth to tell Andrew to stay out of her business, but now that she'd been interrupted, her courage faded.

Andrew's smile met her gaze, and he lifted a French fry and dipped it into ketchup he'd squirted on the edge of his plate. "I know these aren't healthy, but then most pleasurable things are usually neither healthy nor wise."

A look flashed over his face that Hannah didn't understand. She only nodded at his comment and lifted the large burger, trying to look like a lady. Despite her efforts, the juice ran down her chin. Embarrassed, she laughed and pulled the sandwich away.

Andrew came to her rescue with his napkin, dabbing at the telltale splotch. His touch pleased her, yet put her on edge. She grasped her knife and cut the burger in two. "Better," she said, realizing her hands trembled as she grasped the bun.

He grinned, then became thoughtful while Hannah concentrated on her burger and tried to calm her wandering thoughts.

"I'll check around," Andrew said, using his fork to cut into his cod. "Don't worry. I'll find something."

Hannah wasn't worried. *She* would find something. "Andrew, I appreciate all you've done for me, but—"

"Don't thank me, Hannah," he said, his face filled with purpose. "I'll find you a place that's perfect."

Hannah opened her mouth to refute him, then closed it again. Her determination had apparently met its match.

Chapter Five

The judge's voice still rang in Hannah's ears as she left the courtroom—thirty days and a two-hundred-dollar fine. That and the judge's personal protection order after Jack's release alleviated her fear. She had a full month to move. Today was April twenty-eighth, and she had until the end of May. She could start her new job without waiting for Jack to pop up unexpectedly and start his terror all over again. Her life was beginning to change for the better.

Past police records, Carla's testimony, and the reports and photos from Loving Arms provided all the evidence needed. The whole proceeding had lasted only a couple of hours, and Hannah felt grateful that for once Jack hadn't talked his way out of serving jail time. He'd done it before with his empty promises and had gotten probation. Jack's promises were lies.

Today, Hannah's heart lifted, and she looked at her watch, pleased she had time to spare; she headed toward Loving Treasures. Annie had learned about an apartment above the shop that would soon be available and would meet Hannah's needs. After pondering Andrew's insistence, Hannah had decided moving could be a positive step.

The bell tinkled over the shop door when Hannah entered, and she stood a moment looking around the boutique. She'd passed the store many times but had never ventured inside. Twenty dollars for a silk scarf seemed pricey, though she knew many people found the purchase commonplace. A woman's greeting sailed across the room, and Hannah pivoted left toward the checkout counter before realizing the voice came from her right.

"May I help you?" the woman asked.

Hannah appraised the clerk. She wore a long purple skirt in crinkle-crepe. Beneath the hem, Hannah noticed a pair of silver sandals offering a view of magenta-painted toenails. A flowered top with flowing sleeves gave the illusion that the woman had stepped off a ship from the Pacific Islands. The only thing missing was a lei.

"I'm Hannah Currey," she said, extending her hand to the lady.

"Hannah," the woman said, gliding across the room to grasp her hand. "I was expecting you. I'm the owner, Claire Dupre."

"This is nice," Hannah said, scanning the room again while not knowing where to begin.

"Annie mentioned you're looking for an apartment."

"Yes. I suppose Annie told you I need to move from my present location." She waited for Claire to say how sorry she was for Hannah's troubles, but the woman only smiled, leaving Hannah wondering if Annie had told her about Jack.

"It's no fun," Claire said, her face registering no concern. "I've been packing and getting organized. My new place will be ready in a couple of weeks—the first house I've owned in such a long time."

"Congratulations," Hannah said, wondering if she would ever have a real home of her own and not just an apartment.

Claire pointed her index finger toward the ceiling. "I've lived up there since I arrived in Loving. It was convenient, but I'm getting older, and lugging groceries up those stairs is wearing me out. Now I'll have a nice ranch. Everything on one level."

Hannah grinned, waiting for Claire to suggest she look at the apartment. Instead, Claire shifted to a display table and sorted through the silk scarves until she located one and drew it from the stack.

"This will look beautiful with your coloring. The rusts and browns draw attention to your eyes, and it's attractive against your beige top." She flared the scarf and drew it around Hannah's neck, then tied it in a loose knot. "Look how lovely," she said, shifting Hannah to a mirror in the center of the display table.

Hannah had no questions about how the woman ran a successful business. She found it difficult to avoid listening to Claire's compliments. "It's very nice, but I'm not in a position to purchase—"

"Purchase?" Claire drew back, a frown washing away her smile. "It's a gift. It is obviously meant for you."

"I can't accept a gift," Hannah said, trying to untie the bow.

"Please," Claire said, her expression intent as she patted the scarf back into place. "I love to give gifts. Don't spoil my day."

Hannah had second thoughts about her shrewd business sense. If the woman gave away her merchandise, her business savvy left something to be desired.

Claire shifted and motioned toward the doorway from which she'd appeared earlier. "I know you're not here to shop. You'd like to see the apartment."

Before Hannah could answer, Claire sashayed across the room, beckoning her to follow. Passing through the doorway, Hannah noted a door to the outside and another to a workroom. On the left a staircase ascended to the second floor.

"You're young enough to handle these stairs without a problem," Claire said, puffing as she took each step.

At the top, she paused, drawing in a deep breath. "When I first came here, these stairs didn't wear me out one bit." She unlocked the door and pushed it open, then motioned inside. "Here it is."

Hannah stepped into the apartment and surveyed a cozy kitchen.

"I'd intended to leave the apartment unoccupied," Claire said. "I didn't want a stranger living above the shop, but Annie told me what a sweet woman you are and mentioned your darling little boy. It just seemed God's plan."

God's plan. Hannah thought the move was Andrew's plan, although a wise one the way things had turned out. "I don't want to trouble you. You're very generous, but if you prefer not to—"

"No. I prefer to rent it to someone like you. Having you here will mean someone's keeping an eye on the store…not that anything has happened, but you never know." She sent Hannah a bright smile. "If you hear strange noises in the night, you can call the police."

Hannah had had enough of the police. Calling them

was the last thing she wanted to do. Hannah turned her gaze from Claire to the kitchen. Though galley-style, it felt roomy enough, and a round table sat in an alcove with seating for four.

"It's nice," she said, running her hand along the neat oak cabinets and pastel-blue countertops. Her focus settled on the stove.

Claire must have noticed. "I'll be leaving all the appliances. The new house comes with them, so it seemed a good idea. Everything here is fairly new. Philip Somerville had this place spiffed up when I moved here."

The name surprised Hannah.

"He always pooh-poohed it, but I'd bet my teeth he did."

She lifted her hand to her mouth as if resetting her dentures, and Hannah feared she had contemplated taking them out and showing them to her. Hannah turned away, fingering the silky scarf around her neck.

"Go ahead and see the rest," Claire said, stepping back to let Hannah go through the doorway.

Hannah wandered into the living room. Sunlight streamed in from the side and front windows, making the room bright and cheery. She followed the opening on the right that led to a short hall with three doors: two bedrooms and a bath. Perfect for her and JJ.

"It's very clean," Hannah said. "Even the carpet looks perfect."

"One person banging around these rooms doesn't give it much wear." She sent Hannah a smile. "Do you like it?"

Like it? Hannah loved it. She'd had to deal with stairs at her other apartment, too. That didn't bother her, and this seemed more private. More like a home. "I like it very much, but I'm not sure I can afford—"

"You can live here free if you pay the utilities."

"Free! I wouldn't think of doing that. No. I'd want to pay a fair rent."

Claire frowned. "What are you paying now?"

Hannah told her, and Claire's face brightened. "Knock a hundred dollars off that, and it's a deal."

"A deal? But why do you want less for—"

"You'll have the utilities, too. Electric and water are set up independently—everything except the heat. We share the same furnace so I'll pay the gas bill." Claire stepped forward and extended her hand. "Please say yes. You'd make me very happy."

Hannah didn't understand, but she didn't question what seemed like a miracle. As frustrated as she was with God, He sometimes opened doors and windows Hannah had never expected. She knew the Bible said His grace was sufficient. Maybe it was.

Hannah grasped Claire's hand. "Thank you so much. The decision to leave my present location has been difficult for me, but I'm glad I made it."

"Wonderful. You can move in any time after May eleventh. The place will be empty."

"Perfect," Hannah said, knowing Jack would still be in jail then. She halted before asking the question that hung in her mind. "Did Annie explain about my move?"

Claire's eyes glanced upward as if thinking. "Well she mentioned you're starting a new job at Loving Chocolate. That's right up the street." Her brows lifted as if waiting for Hannah to respond.

"Yes, I begin in a couple of more weeks." She released Claire's hand, figuring that Annie hadn't told the woman anything about her troubles with Jack, but one day, Hannah knew, she would have to be honest. She wondered if Claire would be as excited about her new tenants when she learned the truth.

Andrew lowered the chair onto the carpet, then stretched his back. "Once Dave and Bob get the sofa up the stairs, that's about it." He surveyed the large room now filled with furniture. "What do you think?"

Hannah turned from the window, her face stressed, eyes tired. "I'm amazed you rounded up so many men from your church to help move my things, and then Annie called and said her husband Ken had volunteered, too."

"Better a bunch of men moving furniture than you, and it's wiser. No one, except Carla, knows where you are, and I think she'll keep that from Jack when he's released."

"And then I have the protection order."

"Let's hope you won't need it. You'll have moved and have the new job by the time he's released."

Hannah's shoulders lifted in a sigh. "It still scares me. If he does find me, I don't want him coming here and making a scene like he did at Loving Arms, and I haven't told Claire anything yet."

Andrew shook his head. "The news will roll right off her back. She's not a woman to let problems upset her."

"How do you know Claire so well?" Hannah asked.

"She's Jemma's former mother-in-law. Her son died young and left Jemma a widow. She came to Loving when Claire moved back here."

"Claire mentioned knowing Philip." Hannah brushed a strand of hair from her cheek. "I hope you're right about Claire not getting upset when I tell her."

"If anyone can handle a difficult situation and turn it into something positive, it's Claire."

"I know Claire's generous. She tied a scarf around my neck right off the display counter and wouldn't give up until I accepted it."

Andrew's gaze lowered to Hannah's slender neck, and he felt a stirring in his gut. "I've heard that about Claire." At least, being an unmarried man had saved him from Claire's penchant for giving away her merchandise.

A noise from the hallway captured Andrew's attention, and he hurried to the doorway in time to hold it open for two men to wrestle in the sofa. Behind them, Ken struggled with an armchair.

"This baby is big," Bob said as he and Dave maneuvered it to the bare wall. "Here?" he asked.

"That looks great," Hannah said. "I can't thank you enough."

"No problem," Dave said.

Ken hefted the chair toward the sofa. "How's this?"

Hannah gave him a thumbs-up. "It looks good."

He patted the cushion into place and did a full turn, eyeing the room. "Looks like you're all set."

"Yes, thanks." Hannah dug into her pocket and pulled out some bills. "This isn't much but I'd like to—"

Andrew watched the three men lift their hands in protest.

"No ma'am," Dave said. "This is our way of doing for others as we would have them do for us."

"The Golden Rule," Bob added. "One day we might ask you to move our furniture."

Ken grinned. "You've babysat enough for Annie over the last couple of weeks that I owe you a move all by myself."

"Thanks to both of you for the use of your trucks," Andrew added. "We couldn't have done it without those."

"You're welcome," Ken and Bob said as the men headed toward the kitchen. Andrew followed, thanking them again. When he saw the outside door close at the bottom of the stairs, he shut the apartment door and returned to the living room.

"You should probably keep your door locked," he said, hating to mention his worry. "You don't want a customer wandering up here." Or Jack, once he's free, he thought.

"I will." She gestured toward the kitchen counter. "I made some coffee. Would you like a cup?"

"Sure," Andrew said, sinking into the chair and observing her as she pulled mugs from the cabinet. She stood on tiptoe to reach the second shelf, and Andrew's gaze was drawn to her slender form. Short and sweet, he thought with a grin.

"I'm glad I got some of these things put away yesterday," Hannah said. "It makes getting settled so much easier."

"And you have your car again." When his comment registered, he realized she wouldn't need rides anymore. The thought gave him an empty feeling.

Andrew's gaze drifted around the small apartment. "Hannah, have you realized there's no yard here and no place for JJ to play? That's not good."

As the pungent scent of coffee sailed from the maker, Hannah set the mugs on the table. "The other apartment didn't have a yard, either. I can take him to the park, and I'm saving money on rent—Claire has been so kind— I talked with Christie Hanuman at Loving Care about sending JJ there a couple days a week. Her childcare facility has swings and a nice playground. Then in the fall, he'll start kindergarten."

"I know Christie Hanuman. She's a member of my church," Andrew said. But he left thinking of the child's predicament, which wasn't his business. He needed to face facts. Hannah had handled life before he'd come along. Why did he think she couldn't deal with it now?

Hannah poured coffee into the mugs, then offered him cream and sugar, but he declined and stared into the black liquid. There were so many things he wanted to know about her.

He opened his mouth, then closed it. A direct question wouldn't sit well with Hannah. Not now, and he let his mind drift to a new subject. "Are you ready for the new job tomorrow?"

Hannah concentrated on pouring the milk into her coffee before she answered. "I'm not sure *ready* is the word, but I am grateful. I used to love making candy, and it was pretty good if I do say so myself. Good candy has to do with temperature and consistency—but it's been years. Jack didn't—"

Andrew tightened his jaw, seeing the look on her face. Jack had destroyed her creativity, her security, her life.

"I'm grateful for Jenni's job offer, and I'll be fine once I get started again."

Her expression grew serious with the conversation, but Andrew had gotten stuck on the sentence about Jack that she'd cut short. Again he was curious, but didn't ask.

As quickly as her face brightened, it faded again. "I'll have to tell Jenni about Jack. It's only fair."

Andrew wondered about the wisdom of telling Jenni. He knew Jenni Bronski from church, and the resort had ordered her chocolates for special events, but she might not be as willing to deal with those kinds of problems as Claire would be. Maybe if Hannah waited until she'd established herself at the candy shop. He opened his mouth to caution her.

"You probably think I should wait, but I'd rather get it over with. I can always go back to the salon if need be."

Andrew put a cap on his thought. "You do whatever you have to." He rested against the chair back, sensing her resistance.

Silence fell between them while Andrew recalled something he'd thought about earlier that day. "When I stopped by the church this morning to meet the guys, I noticed a flyer about our congregational picnic. It's the Sunday before Memorial Day."

She didn't respond, and he figured her mind was still tangled around talking with Jenni.

"Do you like picnics?"

She raised her head and looked at him. "It depends."

Her comment stymied him for a moment.

Then she chuckled. "I remember church picnics when I was a kid. They were fun. The kids ran races. I remember the bag race and carrying eggs on a spoon. My neighbors were a Christian family and took me a few times."

That was another thing Andrew wondered about. She'd never volunteered information about her family, and he'd avoided asking. "Kids like picnics." He lifted his drink and took a sip. "Do you think JJ might like to go?"

"JJ?"

"You and JJ, naturally," Andrew said. "It's held at the lighthouse park. Free hot dogs, soda and ice cream."

"I'm not sure—" Hannah said. She hesitated, then glanced at the kitchen clock. "I have to pick up JJ in a few minutes. Annie's been so good about entertaining him. I'm so grateful she and I have become friends."

She didn't give him an answer, and to Andrew the wait felt like an eternity. He sensed it was time he left.

"I'm not very comfortable in crowds," Hannah said. "Let me think about it, okay?"

"Sure," he said, scooting back the chair and rising. "I just figured it would be nice for JJ."

She only nodded, and he turned to the door, opened it and waved as he walked out.

Chapter Six

Hannah pushed the hairnet back from her forehead and eyed the temperature gauge. The chocolate aroma rose from the large kettle as nausea overcame her. She'd been stressed out since testifying at Jack's court proceeding, close to three weeks before and it was too early in the day to cope with the candy's pungent odor.

Knowing the pot needed only a couple of more minutes, she moved to the next burner and tilted the thermometer so she could read the degrees. She gave the chocolate pellets a stir, sure they needed more time, then crossed the room away from the heat. She'd become confident with the new job since she'd begun employment there a week earlier.

Perspiration beaded her temples as she waited for the chocolate to melt. Though the kitchen was air-conditioned, the temperature from the outside and the large ranges thwarted the air conditioner's effectiveness.

Hannah wandered into the alcove and opened the freezer, swinging it back and forth for air while the late-May sun hammered against the windows.

Closing the freezer door, she shifted to the counter across the room to ready the chocolate molds. She paused to swallow the bitterness that rose to her throat and prayed she wasn't getting ill. The queasy feeling had hit her around the time of Jack's hearing.

As she worked, her mind sought refuge from the humid kitchen. She hadn't seen Andrew since Saturday, but he'd entered her mind more than once. Why she'd balked at his invitation for the church picnic still clogged her thoughts. His interest concerned JJ and had nothing to do with her. Maybe that was the problem.

Hannah had no idea where her feelings began and ended. Andrew had stepped out of the night and become her knight in shining armor, except her knight's armor was a cream-colored sedan. Her thoughts faded when she realized she'd chased him away with her lack of enthusiasm for his invitation.

Why hadn't she agreed to go to the picnic? She didn't like crowds, because she sensed she wasn't as educated or as polished as other people, but she knew that money didn't determine a person's value. Andrew treated her like gold.

The scent of chocolate signaled her senses, and she hurried across the room, fanning herself with potholders, to lift the chocolate from the huge double boiler. Hot water dripped on her foot as she moved the pan toward the molds. She set the pot in a hot-water bath, then worked quickly to stir in the macadamia nuts and dried Michigan cherries. As she began filling the molds, Jenni came through the doorway.

"How's it going?" Jenni asked, dropping her purse on a folding chair near the door.

"Fine," Hannah said, praying the nausea would vanish. "You can check the other double boiler if you would."

"Sure thing." Jenni crossed to the range. "Not too long now." She wandered back to Hannah's side and lifted the finished molds and placed them on a large tray. "I hate to admit this, but hiring someone to help out in the kitchen was a difficult decision."

"Really?" Hannah said, glancing toward her to see if she were joking. "In this heat, I'd be happy to give it up if I were in your shoes."

Jenni chuckled and glanced down at her feet. "Not these shoes. My feet are swollen."

Hannah looked at Jenni's ankles below the hems of her capri pants and saw a slight swelling. She lifted her gaze to Jenni's smile.

"I'm pregnant," Jenni said. "I can't believe it."

Hannah felt her face twist to puzzlement. "Why can't you believe it? You already have one child."

"Cory's my sister's boy. She died when he was three."

Tenderness washed over Hannah as her heart gave a jolt. "I'm sorry. I didn't know about Cory."

Jenni stepped closer and pressed her hand against Hannah's arm. "No problem. I love Cory like my own child."

"He seems like a great kid, and I'm really happy for you and Todd," Hannah said, still curious about why Jenni had been surprised.

"I have endometriosis," Jenni said, answering her unspoken question, "and never thought I'd have a child. Learning I was expecting convinced me to hire you. I need to rest more than I had been."

"Congratulations." Hannah sent her a genuine smile. "I remember when I was pregnant with JJ. I was so excited and amazed at all the changes in my body and my thinking. Being a mother is unspeakable joy, especially when you thought it was impossible."

Jenni put her arm around Hannah and gave her a hug. "Now before we ruin two pots of chocolate, we'd better get to work."

They both fell silent and concentrated on filling the molds and tapping them against the counter to dispel the air bubbles. After the chocolates cooled in the refriger-ator, Hannah decorated the tops with a special mark to indicate the bonbons' flavors.

But the longer Hannah worked, the more queasy she became. When she finished the batch, she headed to the bathroom and turned on the tap, fearing Jenni would send her home. Hannah needed every penny she could get in order to live.

She grasped a paper cup and swallowed some water, hoping to wash down the horrible feeling. Finally she drew up her shoulders and opened the door, determined to make it through the day.

When she stepped back into the kitchen, Cory had come through the back door, his voice enthusiastic about something happening at their church.

"It's our congregational picnic," Jenni said, noticing her bewildered look. "Cory's getting anxious."

Andrew's invitation zoomed through Hannah's mind. "Do you go to United Christian Church?"

"Yes. Do you?"

"No, I don't—I had an invitation to go to the picnic."

"Please come," Jenni said. "It's a great time. They have games for the kids and hot dogs. Even the adults participate in some games. I'd love you to come along. The people are so nice."

"Andrew Somerville invited me." Hannah let the words fly, wondering what Jenni would say.

She didn't react. "Then you should join us. The picnic's next Sunday. I'll be disappointed if you don't make it."

Hannah grinned and lifted the decorator bag filled with white chocolate, then made the signature design on the candies. Andrew hadn't called her since his invitation, and she wondered if he would.

JJ sprang across the kitchen door, and Hannah grabbed the jamb to keep from tripping over him. "Slow down." She grasped his shoulder and drew him to her side. "Are you ready?"

He nodded, a bright smile on his face. "We're going on a picnic with Andrew. We're going on a picnic with Andrew." He sang the words over and over until Hannah wanted to muzzle him, but she also felt the surge of excitement followed by a hint of uneasiness.

By the time Andrew had finally called on Thursday, Hannah had convinced herself he'd never call again. The resort manager had gone on vacation, and Andrew had been extremely busy, he'd said. Hannah wondered if it was only that or was it her rejection that had kept him away.

Whatever his reason, she decided to attend the church function and enjoy herself. She knew Jenni and her family now, and perhaps she'd see others that she knew from town.

After accepting the picnic invitation, guilt had crept into her thoughts. If someone asked her where she attended church, she'd have to tell the truth and say nowhere. Though she'd attended years ago, when she'd married Jack, her life had become so unsettled and her body had been so often aching with bruises she'd avoided worship. She'd avoided God, as well.

Hannah didn't like to think about her old attitude. Before Jack moved out, she'd asked herself why God let bad things happen to good people. But today she realized that many times problems led to something wonderful. If she hadn't walked out that stormy night, she would never have met Andrew.

Andrew's familiar knock tapped on the door, and Hannah headed for it, avoiding another collision with JJ. When she pulled open the door, JJ was at the screen handle before she could invite Andrew inside.

"Ready?" he asked.

"I'm ready," JJ said, stepping back to show Andrew what he was wearing.

Andrew stood, arms akimbo, while he inspected JJ's outfit, head to toe. "You're lookin' good, JJ." He lifted his gaze to Hannah and scanned her from head to toe. "You're looking good, too."

She felt gooseflesh roll up her arms. "Thanks. I'm ready, but I need to get the food."

"You're speaking to a man's heart with those words," he said, following her toward the kitchen.

"I made a pasta salad and a fruit bowl. Does everyone share or—"

"They share," he said. "They have a long table where everyone adds to the potluck."

"That's what I'd hoped." She opened the refrigerator and lifted out a large plastic bowl filled with salad and another with fruit.

Andrew grasped one container from the counter. "You're feeding an army?"

"I assumed you have a big congregation," she said,

picking up the other bowl. She felt nervous and despised the feeling.

Andrew went on ahead of her, and she paused to lock the door. When she reached the car, Andrew had already made sure JJ had hooked his seat belt. She slid into the passenger side and held the bowl in her lap.

When they reached the highway, Andrew glanced her way. "I'm sorry I haven't called. It's been hectic as I said. I have another week of this before Ian returns."

She hid her disappointment, recalling how much she'd missed Andrew during the past week.

"How's the job?" he asked.

She filled him in on what she'd learned, but her heart wasn't in the telling. She had so many things she wished they could talk about. Instead, they talked about truffles and bonbons.

Hannah saw the lighthouse glint in the afternoon sun as they came from behind a line of trees. Its red missile shape jutted above the long pier while waves glinted as they rolled onto shore and dragged the sandy beach back into the Lake Michigan water.

"We're here," JJ called from the back seat.

"Just about," Hannah said, turning around to give him a smile. Seeing JJ smile so broadly was a rare treasure, and exhilaration soared through her. Andrew had not only been their knight that first evening, but also he'd brought new happiness into their lives.

The notion made Hannah's stomach twitch again, and the gnawing feeling she'd had so often pressed upon her. She feared she'd developed an ulcer from the stress she'd faced recently.

Andrew turned into the park and found an empty space. He pulled the sedan into it, turned off the ignition and hurried around to unlatch JJ. As he reached the door, his cell phone sang out.

The call captured Hannah's curiosity, and she feared he'd been called back into work for an emergency. She tried not to listen, but he didn't lower his voice and soon she knew he was talking to his brother.

"Do you need me now?" Andrew asked.

Hannah's chest tightened, waiting.

"Okay, but if you do just give me a call. I'll tell everyone what's up. Tell Jemma to hang in there." He clicked off and dropped the phone into his pocket.

"Work problems?" Hannah asked.

He gave a quick head shake. "Jemma's gone into labor."

"Then you have to leave?" A twinge of disappointment followed her comment.

"No, but I will do this." He tilted his head heavenward. "Lord, be with Jemma and Philip and give us a healthy baby whatever it may be."

Hannah heard herself join in the "Amen." It seemed so natural, and Andrew's prayer seemed like he was having a conversation with an old friend. "Are you sure you want to stay here?"

"They don't need me now, but he'll call if he does."

"Should we go back and pick up Ellie? She'll miss all the fun."

Andrew touched her cheek. "Thanks, but no. Look at JJ. He's already tugging on you."

Hannah tousled JJ's hair and gave him a squeeze. "He's never been to a picnic like this before."

Opening the trunk, Andrew gave her a wink. "Then it's time he was." He unloaded two lawn chairs and one of the plastic dishes, then steered her toward the folding tables stretched out beneath a tree, laden with salads and desserts. The smell of hot dogs rose from the grills, and nausea rose in Hannah's throat. The sick feeling dampened her spirit.

As people dropped by to greet Andrew, he introduced her, and before long, Jenni arrived. JJ had already found a friend, and Hannah's excitement soared, watching her son run off with the boy toward a ring-toss game where the children were taking turns trying to circle the peg. A group of teens had set up a croquet set while the adults relaxed in lawn chairs in the shade of a large elm.

More introductions left Hannah in a whirl of names and faces she would never remember. The voices and laughter echoed above the sound of the waves splashing onto the shore.

The meal began with prayer, and soon families and friends gathered around the long table to fill their plates. Jenni, her husband Todd and Cory settled at Hannah's picnic table.

Jenni talked about her business, and the conversation moved from chocolates to Bay Breeze, then the church as they ate. When the children became restless, the games finally began.

"How about a walk?" Andrew said, once the others had moved their chairs to watch the children's competitions.

"Sounds good," Hannah said, happy to get up and move around to ease her discomfort.

She let Jenni know they were taking a walk, and Jenni promised Hannah she'd keep an eye on JJ. Andrew took her arm and led her away from the others. He guided her toward the trees rising in the distance away from the water.

They walked in silence, and Hannah's gaze followed

the dance of sunshine through the branches, mesmerized by the dappled design shimmering on the grass. The day seemed near perfect.

"Thanks for inviting me," Hannah said, breaking the quiet. "I'm usually not comfortable with strangers. I never have much to say."

Andrew drew back. "Why? You have a lot to offer the conversation."

"Me?" His comment surprised her, and she faltered.

He slid his arm around her back. "Were you always shy?"

The sensation sent a quiver through her chest. His gentle touch surprised her. "I'm not really shy," Hannah said, immediately realizing she'd opened a door she preferred closed.

"So what is it then?"

She'd done as she'd feared. The words caught in her throat. "It's the way I was brought up." She hoped the explanation would suffice.

He stopped and motioned toward a bench beneath the trees with a view of the lake. "I've often wondered about your family. You don't talk about them."

Bile rose in her throat again, and she wished she'd just agreed she was shy. "They're long gone. I don't hear from my sister. We all scattered across the country years ago."

"That's too bad."

It wasn't bad at all in Hannah's mind. She had felt relief being free from their troubled lives. When she looked into Andrew's eyes, she felt a nudge to be honest. If her background was going to chase him away, then she'd better reveal it now before she had too much at stake in their friendship.

Hannah drew in a lengthy breath. "My folks were

poor, Andrew. My dad drank himself to death, and my mom wasn't a strong woman, though she was a Christian and tried to protect us. She died ten years ago. My brother Bill died in a drunk-driving accident. He ran into a tree. My sister ran off with her boyfriend. Last I heard she'd married someone else. That's about it." The words came out in a rush, and her lungs felt depleted.

"I didn't realize," he said, looking at her with tenderness and not the scorn that she'd expected.

She calmed her thoughts. She'd told him the truth and now he knew. "But I refuse to let that affect me. I found a job to support myself and I got away from home. I wanted control of my life. That's still my goal. I want to be the best mom I can be. JJ is my joy, and I'll fight anything or anyone who tries to harm him."

"You're a great mother, Hannah. Sometimes troubles make us stronger. We put things in perspective and find priorities," Andrew said.

"JJ's my priority."

Something behind his look sent her an uncomfortable feeling.

Andrew rose and reached for her hand. She offered it to him and felt the strength of his larger palm against hers as they headed back the way they had come. Quiet settled around him except for the birdcalls echoing through the trees and the waves surging to shore.

"Why did you marry Jack?"

The question flew out of the silence, and Hannah let her hand slip from Andrew's. Jack had been one of her bad decisions, a failing that she longed to forget. "I was foolish. There's no other reason."

"Was he abusive from the start?"

"Not really. Rougher than some, I suppose, but it

seemed more playful. I knew he drank, but I didn't know it was a problem. It seemed right at the time. I'd gotten laid off from my job. I felt purposeless and alone. Jack walked into my life with lots of promises and seemed the answer to my prayers. Obviously I was wrong."

Andrew didn't respond, and as she studied his face, Hannah felt on edge at the look in his eyes.

Chapter Seven

Andrew's gut tightened when Hannah gave him a puzzled look. Now would be the perfect time to tell her about his past, but something kept him from revealing it. She'd never asked about his past so Andrew assumed she still hadn't heard the rumors. He sensed she respected him as a man with a future. Why would he want to chase her away by revealing his own bad decisions?

The situation struck him. Hannah had become more than a casual friend to him. His brain told him she was a woman who needed someone, but his heart made him face the fact that he longed for her as a special woman in his life, and if anything were to come of their relationship, he would have to admit his failures.

But Andrew closed his mouth and stifled his admission. He looked into Hannah's concerned eyes. "I'd never think less of you. Trust me. The Bible says we shouldn't judge unless we want to be judged. I understand that at times we all make decisions we feel are justified. Sometimes we're wrong."

Hannah blinked as if his comment surprised her.

Before he opened his mouth to explain, his cell phone chimed, and remembering Philip's earlier call, he grabbed the phone from his pocket.

Philip's voice came through the line. "It's Jemma. She's in hard labor. Can you take care of Ellie until Claire can close the store and get over here? I hate to ruin the picnic."

"The picnic? What's more important than you and Jemma? I'll be there as fast as I can."

"Is it Jemma?" Hannah asked, her eyes inquiring as she kept pace with his brisk strides.

"He asked me to watch Ellie. They need to leave for the hospital. Do you mind catching a ride home with Jenni?"

"I'd like to go with you if you don't mind."

Her response surprised him. "Not at all, but what about JJ?"

"He'll come along." She sounded breathless. "Maybe I can help with Ellie."

He didn't argue and liked the idea of having her company. The excitement of the new baby kicked in, and he kept his strides fast and steady until they returned to the picnickers.

Hannah hurried away to find JJ while Andrew packed up the chairs and the items Hannah had brought. Soon Hannah returned with a pouting son, and Andrew couldn't blame the boy. JJ didn't want to miss the fun.

"Are you sure?" he asked Hannah, tilting his head toward JJ.

She nodded. "I'm sure. He'll be fine when he meets Ellie."

Andrew didn't ask again. He hurried them back to the car with the picnic gear and headed for Philip's. When

Andrew pulled in front of his brother's house, the door flew open, and Philip darted outside with a small suitcase. "We've waited too long," he called in passing.

Philip's words fell like a weight in Andrew's gut, and he eyed Jemma who stood in the doorway, kissing Ellie goodbye. He could see the pain on her face and the stress in her posture.

Though Ellie whined at her mother's leaving, she changed her attitude when Andrew called hello.

"Unkie And'woo." She opened her arms, beaming a sweet smile and ran toward him as his chest knotted.

"We'll be fine," he said to Jemma who hadn't moved from the porch. "This is Hannah Currey and JJ. They've come to help."

"Nice to meet you," Jemma said, trying to look pleasant when she was obviously in distress.

"You'd better be on your way," Hannah said, waving them off. "We can visit some other time."

Jemma gave her a weak smile and hugged Andrew. "Thanks. Claire should be here in an hour or so."

Philip helped her down the porch steps, his look tense, and hovered over her as Jemma slid into the sedan.

Andrew cuddled Ellie in his arms, wrapped in her unconditional love, so unlike much of his life. When Philip's car had disappeared down the highway, Andrew pushed open the door and beckoned Hannah to enter.

JJ gave a curious look at Ellie. "Can she talk?"

Andrew chuckled. "She talks up a storm, JJ, and she has some pretty nice toys, too."

Hannah shooed him inside and followed.

"Girl toys?" JJ asked charging ahead.

Andrew shut the door and strode into the living. "Not all girl toys. She has blocks and books."

"Blocks," Ellie said, squirming to get down. "Let's play." She charged across the room and opened a wooden bench beneath the window. A large bag of building blocks tumbled to the floor.

JJ only took a minute to dart across the room and collapse into the midst of them.

"Have a seat," Andrew said to Hannah while she stood back near the archway.

Her eyes shifted as she took in the room, then she ambled in and sat on the sofa. "They have a pretty house," she said, running her hand across the upholstery. "This is expensive."

Andrew shrugged. "It's Jemma's taste, I think. She likes the antiques and sturdy pieces of furniture. When Philip lived at the resort, he had contemporary. Nice, but nothing this fancy." He gestured toward the grandfather clock and the seating arrangement around the fireplace.

"How you doing?" Andrew asked, wandering toward the children. He knelt beside Ellie and brushed hair from her eyes. "Do you know where your mommy went?"

"To bwing a new baby home."

"Right. Did you put in an order? What do you want— a brother or sister?"

She gave the question a lengthy thought as she stacked one block on another before she answered. Finally she giggled. "Just a baby."

"I'm sure you'll get that, my little sugar cake." He patted her cheek.

JJ handed him a block. "Build a fort."

"A fort?" Andrew gave Hannah a silly grin and settled onto the floor, his legs crossed Indian-style.

Hannah watched from across the room, her heart tugging at the sight of Andrew with the children. She had volunteered to come to the house, thinking Andrew might not be comfortable caring for the little girl, but she'd been very wrong. Ellie had run to him as if he were the ice cream man, her arms open and a huge smile on her face. He'd lifted her into his arms with so much love and ease, Hannah knew it hadn't been the first time.

Andrew lined up the blocks, responding to JJ's constant chatter, and Hannah relished the sight of her son with a man who gave him attention. She'd tried to compensate for Jack's disinterest, but nothing could provide a father's love like a father. She realized Andrew wasn't her son's father and never would be, but his manly interest gave JJ something he'd never known before.

Her gaze drifted back to the elegant living room. The blocks and toy bench seemed so incongruous in the lovely surroundings. Jemma had created the perfect conversational setting around the fireplace. Closer to the living-room entrance, the sofa and a chair formed a reading area. Hannah noticed the pile of magazines beneath the table and, on it, a novel with a bookmark placed between the pages.

She glanced again at the children and Andrew, deep in concentration while building the fort. Even Ellie handed him blocks without toppling the creation.

Hannah looked below the table at the magazines and pulled one out. *Architectural Digest.* She flipped through the pages, viewing the elegant homes and furnishing ads. She'd grown up in a house with threadbare upholstery and nicked pine furniture. The pictures on the wall were jigsaw puzzles her mother had placed on adhesive paper and framed. They'd brightened the room, but when the light hit them just so, she could see the grooves and shapes of the pieces.

Hannah's life had been like those puzzle pieces—a blur of colors and patterns that never revealed a clear picture. The picture had become clearer when JJ was born, and at that moment she'd known smoothing the ruts from their lives was her goal. When she'd finally loosened herself from Jack, she'd felt free, but then he'd returned with a vengeance.

She had to keep JJ safe. What could she do to protect him when Jack got out of jail? She had to make changes. She wanted Jack out of her life forever.

Hannah dropped the magazine in her lap, feeling a sudden sense of grief. She had to remain strong. She had to find courage to keep Jack out of her life. She'd met nice people today. They'd treated her as an equal. And she was, Hannah reminded herself. She was a child of God. Even in the midst of their chaotic life, her mother had taught her that. She could still picture Jesus's outstretched arms, inviting her into his embrace. Why did she fight the invitation?

She glanced at her watch. She and Andrew had arrived nearly an hour ago, and now her thoughts turned to Jemma and her labor. Hannah recalled her own labor, which had taken place while Jack sat in a bar. She'd been unable to find him, and a neighbor had taken her to the hospital. Eventually Jack had shown up, his chest bursting with pride that she'd given him a son. He'd insisted he be named after him—Jack Darren Currey, Junior. That was the last day Jack seemed to care about JJ.

Hannah caught herself and stopped her negative thoughts. Andrew had become a special friend. She liked him, and he knew about her past and said he didn't care. She had to learn to trust.

"Anyone hungry?" Andrew asked from across the room.

Though four hours had passed since they'd eaten, Hannah hadn't felt the twinges of hunger. She'd only felt the ever-present gnawing sensation from earlier that day when she'd tried to eat a hot dog at the picnic.

At Andrew's question, Ellie jumped up and clapped her hands while JJ's face brightened at the mention of food. Andrew beckoned to her and slipped through the archway with the two children on his heels.

Hannah took the hint he wanted her help and entered the kitchen. She faltered in the doorway, seeing the expanse of cabinets in rich oak and the striking rust-colored counter tops. Andrew stood beside the center island, reading a note.

"Ready to eat?" His eyes met hers, then waved the scrawled message in her direction. "Jemma says there's plenty in the fridge that she planned for the picnic."

When she opened the refrigerator, Hannah found salads, sliced ham and a scrumptious-looking bakery cake. Andrew joined her, setting the table while she pulled out the food, but as they sat down for supper, the telephone rang, followed by the doorbell.

As Andrew headed for the phone, Hannah hurried to the entrance. As she suspected, Claire stood on the porch, and Hannah grinned at Claire's look of surprise. "I was with Andrew at the picnic when Philip called," she said, explaining before Claire asked.

"Thanks for coming with him," Claire said, sweeping into the room.

"Nana," Ellie cried when Claire stepped into the kitchen.

But when she looked at Andrew's face, Hannah's heart squeezed with concern.

"Claire's here now," Andrew said. "I'm coming up, Philip."

"What is it?" Claire asked as soon as he hung up the receiver.

"Complications. Umbilical cord prolapse, and they're doing a cesarean section."

"No," Hannah moaned, filled with dread. "The baby's been cut off from its oxygen supply."

"If the physician works fast, Philip said, everything will be fine."

Hannah drew in a ragged breath. "But an emergency cesarean isn't good."

Claire gave a knowing nod as if she understood. "She's right, Andrew. You go to your brother, and I'll take over here."

"No, please," Hannah said, "let me stay with the children. Claire, you should go, too."

Claire held up her hand. "I can be helpful with all kinds of problems, but not this one. I'd feel more useful staying here. Hannah, you go with him."

"No. This is a family matter. I can call a cab. You go ahead, Andrew. Please."

Andrew shook his head as he headed for the door. "The hospital isn't that far from your house. I'll drop you off."

"And you'll let me know how—"

He touched her cheek, stopping her words. "You know I'll keep you posted."

Andrew eyed the waiting-room wall clock, then checked his watch. Time seemed to stand still. Philip had paced the floor from the moment Andrew had arrived, and no matter what he said Philip wouldn't sit.

"You're wearing out the carpet," Andrew said. "Let me get you some coffee."

Philip only shook his head. "What's taking so long?"

He strode across the room to the desk, and Andrew's heart broke watching his brother's anguish.

Marriage and family had begun to settle in Andrew's thoughts. He'd always told himself that he had nothing to offer a woman, but Hannah seemed different. She had none of the expectations most people had of the Somervilles. She'd come from a family with so little, yet she'd done her best and made a life of nothing. Why couldn't he do the same?

Hannah always made Andrew smile. He knew why she'd offered to come to Philip's: she'd figured he'd be useless babysitting his niece, but he'd fooled her. He'd seen the surprise on her face when Ellie had bounded into his arms. He didn't want to be cocky, but he'd proved to himself that the past hadn't totally destroyed the love of family. Envy had wheedled its way into his thoughts, but hadn't destroyed the love he still felt for Philip. He'd just had a difficult time showing it.

JJ had been an eye-opener, too. Sure, he figured loving his niece was natural, but loving a child who was no relation, that was another story. But that's what had happened. He found himself doting on the young boy.

Andrew shifted his gaze and noticed a surgeon in the hallway outside the waiting room. Philip seemed to notice at the same time. He darted across the room and met the man before he came through the doorway.

Nailed to his seat, Andrew watched the drama unfold

and finally could no longer contain himself, but rose and joined the two men.

"She's not out of the woods," the physician said.

Fear surged through Andrew. The baby or Jemma? He clamped his mouth closed rather than interrupt their conversation.

"We're doing all we can, but it will be twenty-four hours or more before we can be certain."

"The baby?" Andrew whispered, giving in to his uncontrollable worry.

Philip's head gave a slow shake. "It's Jemma." His voice trembled, and tears sprang to his eyes.

Jemma? Dear Lord, no. Andrew's prayer flew to heaven.

"Your son is in good health," the physician continued. "You can see him in a few minutes. I'll have a nurse let you know." He took a step backward. "I'm sorry, Mr. Somerville. I wish I had better news."

Philip stood frozen in place as the doctor turned and left.

Andrew stared at his brother in disbelief. "What happened?"

"She reacted to the anesthesia and stopped breathing."

Andrew didn't understand, but it wasn't time to ply his brother with questions. He rested his hand on Philip's shoulder.

Philip continued without question. "During an emergency they have to use general anesthesia and that has a risk factor. She went into respiratory arrest."

Respiratory arrest. The words cut through Andrew's heart and his defenses. Without thought, Andrew drew his brother into his arms and embraced him. Philip pressed his face against Andrew's neck and sobbed while tears rolled from Andrew's eyes and joined Philip's.

"Heavenly Father," Andrew whispered through his sorrow, "be with Jemma and hold her in Your healing hand. You can make all things right, and with You, nothing is impossible. Lord, we understand Your will. Your needs are first in our lives, but Father, please remember Ellie and their new son…" A son. The word hadn't sunk in until now. "…their new son who needs a mother so badly, and Philip who wants his wife by his side."

"Thank you," Philip murmured as he pulled back and withdrew a handkerchief from his pocket. He wiped his eyes, then blew his nose and grasped Andrew's hand. "It's good to have you here. This means more to me than anything."

Andrew's thoughts spiraled. *This means more to me than anything.* Could Philip forget? How could he forgive the years Andrew had been away? The time he'd avoided coming home for their father's funeral? Squandering the family money? But the sincerity in Philip's eyes quelled the negative thoughts running through Andrew's mind. "It means more than you know for me to be here, Philip. I love you and Jemma. I've probably never said that before."

"You didn't have to," Philip said. He finally moved from the hallway and returned to the waiting room, but this time he found a chair and sank into it.

Andrew sat beside him, wishing he could think of something to say, but nothing seemed worthwhile except the prayer he'd sent heavenward.

Hannah rose in his thoughts. He needed to call her, but more than the call, Andrew realized that Hannah had become a primary part of his life. Since he'd found her and JJ on the highway, their lives had begun to inter-twine, and Andrew clung to the warm feeling.

Friendship. His jaw tightened. *Friendship* had become too weak a word. *Relationship* didn't seem strong enough. What were they? His pulse picked up speed as he pondered the reality that swept over him. He could no longer dismiss the growing feelings, the emotion that he'd tried to avoid and the longing he'd fought to quell.

Chapter Eight

Propped on her elbow, Hannah clung to the bedroom phone receiver, feeling the worry in Andrew's early-morning call. Though she'd only met Jemma for a moment, she'd heard so many nice things about her, and she knew Jemma was esteemed in the community. She and Philip were strong Christians who didn't deserve such sadness.

She never understood sorrow, except she knew it happened for God's purpose, a purpose she would never understand until she met the Lord face to face.

Andrew's tired voice had dragged through the phone line. He'd called her last evening and again this morning. Anxious to see him, Hannah had offered him breakfast, and he'd agreed to stop by. Needing to get up and make the meal she'd promised, Hannah slipped her feet from beneath the sheet.

The Memorial Day holiday provided Hannah a day to relax. She tiptoed to her son's room, and JJ's silence attested to the fact that he was still sleeping. Hannah reveled in the luxury of stepping into the shower in silence and letting the warm water wash over her tired, tense body while her prayer rose to heaven. "I'm tired of fighting you, Lord," she said aloud, "and I'm sure You're tired of my struggle. Help me to hold on to Your promises, and to learn that You know what's best for us all."

The words left her, yet she asked herself what good could come from Jemma losing her life to bring a new child into the world. It all seemed so unfair, so unbelievably horrible. The ulcer, Hannah suspected racked her belly, and she swallowed the gnawing sensation that had surged through her the past month.

She dressed quickly, checked on JJ again, then strode to the kitchen to prepare coffee. While the maker gurgled and dripped liquid into the pot, she pulled eggs and sausage from the refrigerator.

Andrew deserved a home-cooked breakfast. He'd spent the night with Philip and had seen the sun rise with no change in Jemma's condition as she clung to life. Tears bubbled in Hannah's eyes, and she brushed them away with the back of her hand, amazed she felt so much sorrow for a family she barely knew. Yet she knew Andrew, and she was certain his brother and family were as kind and caring as he was.

With the bacon sputtering in the pan, Hannah whisked the eggs, added milk and some diced onions she'd had leftover from the pasta salad she'd made for the picnic, then she poured the mixture into the frying pan. As the pungent odors filled the room, nausea rose in Hannah's throat. She gagged at the smell, snapped off the burners and darted into the bathroom.

While she hung her head over the basin, longing to stop the horrible sensation, she heard the doorbell ring. She rinsed her mouth and hurried to the door, trying to cover the next wave of nausea surging over her.

"You look tired," she said as Andrew came into the room. "I'm so sorry for—"

He grasped her shoulders, his eyes glazed with exhaustion. "I know. It's been awful." He drew her closer and rested his head against her hair. "Thanks for letting me come by. I needed to talk with someone who'd understand how I feel. I tried to be strong for Philip."

His touch swept over her while his weary body trembled. Hannah did understand. She wished she comprehended her own ailment as well. The thought of having something seriously wrong herself had only been brushed aside by Jemma's battle to live.

She drew back, and Andrew's whiskers brushed against her cheek. "Come into the kitchen," she said, not wanting to let him go. The closeness felt so good and right. "I've probably burned everything."

He followed her, and with relief, she saw that turning off the burners had saved the food. She popped two pieces of bread into the toaster, poured Andrew's coffee, then went to the hallway door to listen.

"I should wake JJ. He's slept late today. If I don't wake him now, he won't sleep tonight."

"I don't want to mess up your routine," Andrew said.

She faltered, then returned to the table. "Today's a holiday. I suppose you forgot that."

He nodded, sadness covering his features.

"I'm glad you came. I'm happy I can do something for you." She dished up his eggs and sausage, then handed him the plate. When the toast popped, she dropped in two more pieces of bread and pushed down the lever. When she turned around, Andrew's head was bowed, and she assumed he was praying.

"Here," she said, handing him a piece of toast when he'd lifted his head. "I'll have another for you in a second."

She took the other piece, sank into a chair and bit into the toast, hoping to hold back her sick feeling. "Tell me what's happened."

"Aren't you going to eat?"

"I'm not hungry," she said, not wanting to alarm him.

Andrew looked at her a moment, his gaze searching hers, then lowered his fork and told her in detail the trials of the previous evening and the bad news Philip had received in the morning.

"Please tell me there's hope?" Hannah said. "I've prayed for her. I want to know what else I can do."

Andrew's gaze deepened with tenderness. "Thanks. Prayer is the answer. Even the doctor said that's the only thing that will get her through."

The prognosis sounded hopeless, but Hannah crammed the fear back into her mind. "We'll pray continually then. Jesus said ask and you will receive. We have to trust His promises."

Andrew slid his hand across the table to hers resting beside her unused coffee cup. He caressed her fingers and brushed her arm with a gentle touch. "I've been doing a lot of thinking."

Her hopes rose. "About Jemma and Philip?"

"Partly, but about me, too, and what this all means."

His gaze captured hers, and she felt her pulse jump at the look in his eyes. She didn't speak, eager to hear what he meant.

"I've been unable to show love to my brother for many years, and last night I held him in my arms while we both cried. Jemma's illness is horrifying, but it has one positive effect." He paused and added, "It brought Philip and me closer together and allowed me to show my love for him."

Hannah turned her hand palm up and grasped his fingers in hers, giving them a squeeze to let him know she understood.

"Mommy."

JJ's call interrupted Hannah's thoughts. She rose and headed toward the hallway, but JJ met her at the kitchen doorway, his pajamas twisted and his hair rumpled from his pillow. A sleepy look filled his eyes.

When he saw Andrew, a puzzled look spread over his face, and he dug his fists into his eyes as if trying to make sure what he saw was real.

"Hi, JJ," Andrew said, putting his hand on the boy's shoulder as he stood beside him. "Want some breakfast?"

JJ nodded. "Did you come over to eat?"

Andrew chuckled, and the sound spread over Hannah like sunshine. "I invited him over because he was at the hospital all night with his brother."

"You have a brother?" JJ asked, sliding onto the chair.

Andrew nodded. "Just one brother. You saw him yesterday. He's Ellie's father."

JJ thought a moment. "I remember. I wish I had a brother."

His words caught Hannah by surprise. JJ had never mentioned wanting a sibling, and in her predicament, Hannah never expected she would have another child. She started to say her thoughts aloud, but faltered. This wasn't the time to talk about babies.

Instead, Hannah dished some egg onto a plate and pushed the lone piece of cold toast back into the toaster to reheat. "Here's your breakfast, JJ."

He didn't look at the food but eyed Andrew. "Will you stay and play with me?"

This time Andrew laughed out loud and ruffled her son's hair. "I have to go to work, JJ. We can play later."

"Okay," JJ said.

"Work?" Hannah asked.

"The resort is open on holidays. I have to take care of a few things, then I want to go back to the hospital."

"But what about sleep?" His tired face filled her with sadness.

He only shrugged and took a drink of coffee. "Sleep's not important today. Family is."

Hannah let the words flood through her. *Family is important.*

JJ finished his breakfast, at least as much as he would eat, and Andrew lingered over his coffee, then pushed his chair back and rose. "I need to get to Bay Breeze. I know everyone's worried there."

"I'm glad you stopped by. I worry about you."

He stepped closer and rested his hands on her shoulders. "You're a wonderful woman, Hannah. Thanks so much for the breakfast and for your prayers."

Her body trembled as she felt him draw her closer. His arms wrapped around her back and pressed her against his chest. She felt small beside him, and his manly scent awakened her senses.

Before he drew back, he pressed his lips against her cheek. "Thank you for being you." He turned and with a wave vanished through the kitchen doorway.

Hannah clung to the chair back, relishing the softness of his lips on her face and the feel of his warm arms encircling her.

* * *

The following Sunday, Hannah looked out the front window for Andrew. He'd asked her to attend worship, and she'd accepted. Her willing agreement surprised her. She'd been away from her faith so long, but with Jemma hanging on through her serious illness and Hannah's own trials, life had taken a new meaning and so had God.

When she saw Andrew's sedan pull into the driveway, Hannah grabbed her handbag. "Ready, JJ?"

JJ ambled into the room, a pout evident on his face. "Why do we have to go to church? I won't have anything to do."

Repentance gripped Hannah. When she'd been young, she'd had an opportunity to know Jesus through her neighbors, but her son had been cheated because she hadn't given him the opportunity to learn. "They have kids' church, JJ. It's fun. You'll do crafts and play." And learn about Jesus, she thought to herself, not wanting to confuse him.

"Will Andrew play, too?"

Andrew. The child's thoughts were so focused on Andrew's presence in their lives. Her heart ached. "Andrew will go to the big people's church with me, but maybe after church we can do something fun. I'll see, okay?"

The doorbell rang in unison with JJ's "Okay." He dragged his feet to the door, but seeing Andrew he perked up. "Can we do something fun after church?"

"I'm sorry," Hannah said, aghast at her son's bold request. She leaned closer to Andrew's ear. "He's not real excited about going to church."

"We'll go out for lunch, JJ. To one of those fast-food places where they have tunnels and slides."

"Yippee," JJ sang as they headed to the car.

"Don't worry about it," Andrew said, putting his arm around Hannah's shoulder. "I wanted to talk with you anyway."

"About Jemma? Is she worse?"

"She's still hanging in there. The more time that passes the better the prognosis, the doctor said. Keep the prayers flying."

"I have."

"I wanted to talk with you about…me."

"You?" Her heart tumbled to her shoes.

"You'll understand, but later, okay?"

She nodded, trying to look unaffected by his words. Had he decided he'd been spending too much time with her? Might he confess he'd met someone else?

They settled into the car with JJ buckled into the back seat and headed for church, both deep in their own thoughts. Hannah sensed that something weighed heavily on Andrew's mind. She saw his tense grip on the steering wheel, his shoulders rigid. The more time that passed without him talking, the more bewildered she became. If he wanted to say goodbye, she wished he'd done it long ago.

In the church parking lot, Hannah stepped into the summer sun, then reached for the back door to help JJ, but Andrew had hurried around the car and taken over. As her son slid to the ground, Andrew grasped Hannah's hand and walked beside her toward the church's side entrance.

Andrew located the proper classroom for JJ, and once her son seemed comfortable, they headed into the church foyer. Beyond the wide arch, the worship area stretched before them already filled with people. Hannah scanned the worshipers, recognizing a few.

As they moved down the aisle, Andrew stopped to answer questions about Jemma's progress and to greet people he knew. He introduced Hannah to those she hadn't met at the picnic until he finally halted and motioned her into a row.

Hannah sat and looked through the church bulletin while her thoughts lingered on Andrew's earlier comment. What did he want to talk about later? The old fear teased her newfound confidence. Her life had been different from Andrew's, and looking around at the well-dressed congregation only shook her assurance further.

The organ began, and the congregation rose to sing. A reader stepped to the podium, and the Bible verses marched through her mind—some familiar, some not. She tried to concentrate on the sermon, but her thoughts wandered, and not until prayer time, when the pastor asked for continued prayer for Jemma and Philip did she truly tune in to the service.

She could only imagine Philip's anxiety, and she longed to be confident that God would make all things right, but she'd prayed years ago and things hadn't gotten any better. Hannah wanted so badly to trust the Lord. Though skepticism nudged at her, she prayed, hoping, longing to have the Lord answer the united prayer of the people who now asked for Jemma's healing.

The service ended, and outside in the sunlight, JJ bounded toward them from the side door. "Let's go to the restaurant," he said, dangling something in his hand.

"What's that," Hannah asked, pointing to the item that fluttered on the breeze.

"It's fruits."

"Fruits?" She reached down and lifted the paper creation he'd made. She turned it over, and saw a banana with the word *peace* printed along the curve.

"Fruits of the Spirit," Andrew said. "I learned the verse in Sunday school and never forgot it. Galatians 5:22-23. The fruits of the spirit are love, joy, peace, patience, kindness, goodness, faithfulness, gentleness and self-control." He captured JJ's shoulder and drew him closer. "And your fruit is peace. That's something we all need."

"Even you?" JJ asked, looking up at him with hero worship that sent Hannah's heart spiraling.

Andrew grinned. "Even me."

"And me," Hannah said, admitting she'd been so far from peace lately she didn't know if she'd recognize it.

JJ giggled and skipped on ahead of them to the car.

During the ride to the fast-food restaurant, Andrew talked about the sermon. What Andrew said made sense, and she wished she'd tuned in more to the pastor's words.

Andrew pulled into the parking lot, and, in moments, they were in line ordering burgers and fries, not what Hannah considered healthy, but JJ loved the choices. He clung to Andrew like plastic wrap, and Hannah had all she could do not to tell him to stop. Seeing her son hurt when Andrew eventually walked away from them would be more than she could bear. He'd been hurt so much already.

JJ ate half his burger and a few fries, then gulped down his pop and asked to go to the kids' play area.

Hannah sat near the window so she could watch him while they finished their food. She had choked down a few bites of her sandwich and sipped her drink, but neither her heart nor her stomach had been in it.

When Andrew didn't bring up the topic, she finally did. "I thought you wanted to talk with me about something."

"I do," he said, his face growing noticeably strained.

Tension built as she reacted to his look. "Is this the dying man's last meal?" She gestured to her plate.

A puzzled look spread over his face, and she realized he hadn't understood her. "I mean is this bad news for me?"

His face seemed to relax for a moment. "I hope not, but it might be my last meal."

Now she felt totally bewildered. "What do you mean?"

"I want to tell you something about myself, Hannah. I think it's important that you know who I really am."

A frown pulled at her face, and she tried to ease it with her flippant comment. "You're Andrew Somerville, respected citizen of Loving, Michigan, and owner of Bay Breeze Resort."

Andrew shook his head. "No. That's my brother, Philip."

His serious look took her aback. "You are real brothers, aren't you?"

"Yes, but I'm the black sheep of the family, Hannah. I guess you haven't heard. I'm the prodigal son who wasted his inheritance and didn't even think enough of the family to come home for his dad's funeral."

His words knocked the breath from her. How could Andrew have been that unloving, that thoughtless? Impossible. "You're kidding me?"

"No. I'm telling you the truth."

She didn't want to know the truth. Andrew's self-description didn't fit the Andrew she knew. "I don't believe you."

"People have been too kind. They've stopped their gossiping and have forgiven me. I just haven't forgiven myself."

"But how could you do that?"

Andrew stared into Hannah's shocked face and asked himself the same question. "Stupidity."

Hannah lowered her gaze and shook her head. "It had to be more than that."

If he was truthful, and he needed to be, it *had* been more than that.

"Why are you telling me this now?" Hannah asked, without waiting for his answer to the other question.

"Because I care about you. Jemma's illness made me think about family and helped put things in perspective. You and I have become good friends, and I think I owe you the truth. You shared your past with me the other day, and I knew it was only right that I do the same."

"But it doesn't fit you."

"Your difficult life doesn't fit you either, but it's the truth, isn't it?"

Hannah turned toward the window as if checking on JJ and nodded.

"About seven years ago," he began, "I decided I wanted a break from the family business. I'd watched my brother pattern his life after my dad's, and it was a life I didn't think I wanted." He halted, facing the truth. "No, it was a life I didn't think I could handle. I couldn't meet Dad's expectations. Philip was the golden son, the one who did everything right."

She turned from the window to face him, her skin pale and her eyes questioning.

"I left and tried business after business, scheme after scheme until I realized I was a failure. Even away from Philip, I'd never be the golden boy my father could admire. When Dad died, I didn't have the courage to come home. I stayed away licking my wounds until I couldn't do it anymore. I came home, humbled and contrite."

"What happened when you came back?"

"That still confuses me. Philip didn't treat me as if he were the biblical prodigal son's older brother. He took on the father's role and killed the fatted calf. He threw a party to welcome me home."

"But that was wonderful, Andrew. It's what the Bible tells us to do."

"But I felt unworthy. Once again, Philip had behaved like my father, exactly as a Christian should. He even gave me a job at the resort and place to stay until I could get settled in my own home. I'm not that perfect, Hannah. Far from it."

She studied his face as if considering his admission, and Andrew wondered if he'd made a mistake in telling her the truth.

Chapter Nine

Hannah's hand trembled as she lifted the spoon to stir the chocolate. Her mind reeled with so many complications, so many overwhelming issues, she no longer knew which way to turn.

Nearly two weeks had passed since Andrew had spoken with her about his past, and that day seemed to have put a wedge between them. She hadn't responded the way he'd needed her to. She knew that, but she'd been so startled by what he'd said; if he'd stumbled once, he could stumble again.

She'd let her heart get wrapped up in a man she didn't know well and one who probably had no real feelings for her. Now she realized that putting her hopes in a man who took wild chances to prove himself could be another step into the path of danger. As questions tumbled in her mind, God's word dashed it away. Do not judge. Be compassionate. Trust in the Lord. Forgive, so the Father can forgive you. So many thoughts that made her ashamed of her behavior.

Miraculously, Jemma had rallied and seemed to be

making good progress. Hannah had rejoiced at the news. Yet Hannah's upset hadn't eased. She pressed her hand against her belly, facing the truth. An ulcer would be a blessing to the real condition she found herself in. Pregnant. She felt certain now. She'd been nauseated, and now she'd missed her third cycle. The first, she'd thought was caused by stress. The second and third...? Why hadn't she realized what the symptoms meant earlier?

"Sorry," Jenni said, dropping some packages on the counter. "I found some new candy boxes at the outlet. I thought we might try them with the chocolate bark. If they work, I can order more from the company at a discount."

Hannah tried to look interested and moved back to stir the pots.

"What's wrong?" Jenni asked, moving to her side.

"Nothing."

"Are you ill?"

Hannah grasped for a response. She couldn't tell Jenni the truth, not now. "I realized the other day that Jack's free again. I'm just edgy."

Jenni gave her a knowing nod. "I figured it was about that time."

"I've done everything I can. I'm working here now. I have the new apartment. Once he begins, JJ's school will be my only problem, but I'll warn them not to release him to anyone without my permission. But Loving's a small town. He'll keep looking. That's Jack."

"You've done what it takes. Did you talk with the police?"

"I did, but they can't do much unless Jack does something first. You know that. What scares me is Jack's persistence. He's like a bloodhound." Goose bumps rose on her arms, remembering a car she spotted yesterday that had resembled Jack's.

Jenni embraced her. "You're safe here, Hannah."

"At least I'm out of the line of vision in the kitchen. That helps, but being at the apartment is another story." Hannah had lots of stories, but none she wanted to share, none she wanted to remember.

On Friday evening, Andrew darted to the side door and hurried up the stairs to Hannah's apartment. He'd called her at work and learned she'd stayed home. Concern dimmed his wonderful news.

At the top of the staircase, he knocked on the door. He waited, then rapped again. No sound came from inside. Recalling that Jack had been released, Andrew faltered while pinpricks of worry stung him. Wondering where she had gone, he turned his back to the door and lowered his foot to the step when he heard a sound. He returned to the landing as the door opened.

Hannah looked at him through the gap in the door.

"What's wrong?" hc asked, as she eased open the door and invited him in.

"I'm not feeling well. It's nothing."

"You look terrible." He glanced around the kitchen and listened for the child's greeting. "Where's JJ?"

"Annie invited him to Gracelynne's birthday party. I'll pick him up later." She searched his face. "Is something wrong?"

"Not at all. I thought you'd want to know that Jemma is coming home today. She's still weak, but Philip and Ellie are so thrilled and the baby needs her."

"That's wonderful news," Hannah said, sinking onto a kitchen chair.

Andrew watched her a moment. Hannah couldn't hide her problems from him anymore. He knew her too well. He pulled out a chair and sat, wondering if he should press her about it. She'd been looking peaked for the past month. Knowing how she hated him to push her into decisions, Andrew held back the urge to suggest she see a doctor. "I suppose I should go. You don't look well."

"I'm okay now. I was feeling ill this morning."

"You really should…" He caught himself and changed the sentence. "…take better care of yourself. You work hard, and you've been under stress." A new worry crossed his mind, and this one he had to ask. "Have you heard from Jack?"

Startled, her gaze latched on to his. "Why are you asking me that?"

"I see something in your eyes. Something more than physical illness. It's fear or worry."

She lowered her head and didn't respond.

"Has he been here, Hannah? Please tell me."

"No, he hasn't been here."

"Outside then?"

She shrugged and rose, crossing to the sink and running a glass of water. She took a sip, then turned back to him. "I think I saw his car on Washington."

"Are you sure?"

A sigh rattled from her chest. "Not positive, but pretty sure. I just sensed it."

"Then you should notify the police."

"But I have no proof. It could be my imagination."

"I doubt that. You know him. You know his car, and you have a protection order to keep him away from you and JJ. Please call the police before he does something."

"If I see him again, I will."

"Promise?"

"Promise," she said.

He rose and pushed in the chair. "Let me drive you to pick up JJ. I don't want you going alone."

"No, I can't live my life in fear. I have to stop for some groceries. I'll be fine. I keep my car doors locked."

He grasped the chair back, wishing he could shake some sense into her. Jack had been volatile, and Andrew had no idea what it might take to set him off again. Laws and court orders wouldn't deter a man like that.

"When are you going for JJ?" Andrew asked.

She glanced at the clock. "I should go now, I suppose."

"I'll walk you out," he said.

He waited until she combed her hair and slipped on a sweater, then went ahead of her down the stairs while she locked the door. Passing the downstairs side entrance into the boutique, he could hear Claire talking with a customer. She'd propped the door open for fresh air, he assumed.

Andrew opened the outside door and held it for Hannah, then watched her climb into her car parked in the back. When she was safe, he dashed to his sedan on the street and waited until she pulled out of the alley onto Washington.

Hannah would be furious if she knew he was following her. She'd been so determined to be independent and stand on her own, but he had a gut feeling that Jack had been on the prowl. As he drove, he kept an eye on the traffic. A dark-blue car moved in behind Hannah's. He recalled Jack's car being that color. His pulse skipped with speculation.

The car stuck to her tail while Andrew stayed two cars behind, keeping an eye on the situation. He saw

Hannah signal for a right turn. The car behind her didn't signal, but when Hannah rounded the curve, the navy-blue car followed.

Andrew's back bristled. He pulled his cell phone from his jacket pocket and stayed back, waiting.

When Hannah pulled to the curb, the other car passed. But Andrew's relief was short-lived. The car made a quick swerve to the side and stopped. Andrew's heart flew to his throat. Jack. He knew it.

He pushed 911 and told the dispatcher what he was witnessing. As Hannah moved away from her car, Jack darted forward and clutched Hannah's shoulders. She pulled away, and her mouth moved as if she were trying to talk sense to him, but Andrew saw tension building. He'd confronted Jack once, and he did not want to get involved again. He would drive Hannah away with his constant interference. He knew that too well.

Instead, he sat with eagle eyes, watching Jack's every move. He could be out of the sedan in a heartbeat if need be, but for now he clutched the steering wheel to keep from running to Hannah's defense.

Hannah tried to pull her shoulder away from Jack's grip, but he seemed to cling like a vise, and Andrew saw Hannah's face wince with pain.

Anger flared in Andrew. He flung open his door just as he saw the police car round the corner. Annie's house door opened, and JJ came bounding outside, distracting Jack. He called to the boy, but JJ hesitated and backed up instead of moving forward.

Jack released Hannah and darted for JJ. The child stood frozen to the ground. Andrew ran forward and grabbed the boy as the police car skidded to a halt. In the midst of the confusion, Andrew hurried with JJ to Hannah's side.

Her eyes widened, and her expression flickered through a multitude of emotions until her face settled into the familiar look of relief and gratitude mixed with irritation, then she ignored Andrew and focused on the officer while he cuffed Jack and pushed him into the police car.

JJ clung to his mother's side, and Andrew knelt to calm the boy. Tears rolled down the child's face and his lip trembled. He put his arms around Andrew's neck and wept into his collar. When he had calmed, Andrew lifted the boy in his arms, keeping the child's vision blocked while the police drove away.

Hannah watched the squad car leave, then turned to Andrew. "What are you doing here?"

"I followed you. I'm sorry."

"Don't do that to me, Andrew. If you do, you're no better than Jack. You just have different motives."

"Hannah, I understand, but don't you see? I care about you and JJ. When I saw the dark-blue car on the street, I couldn't just drive off. I called the police."

Something changed in her eyes, but she stuck to her defiance. "I'm a big girl. What will I do when you're not here to save me? I have to learn to defend myself. I can't depend on others. This is my life."

The sting of her words burned Andrew's cheeks. He was nothing like Jack. He wanted only the best for her, but she couldn't see that. "Would you prefer me to be out of your life?" His heart stopped, hearing his question.

She stared at the ground for a moment, her fingers smoothing JJ's hair. "I don't know what I want, Andrew, but I don't want to be controlled or followed around. I've already had that experience, and I don't like it."

He backed away. He had no intention of controlling her

life. He'd reacted out of Christian love. Christian love? Only that? The time had come to face his real motivation?

"I'm pregnant," Hannah said.

Jenni's mouth dropped open, and a frown altered her usual smile. "But..."

"I know. I'm speechless, too. I'm also depressed."

"Oh, Hannah," Jenni said, her frown fading to tender concern. "I didn't mean to sound—"

"You didn't react any differently than I did when I realized why I'd been so ill. With all this stress, I thought I had an ulcer." Her hand lowered to her growing belly. "I'll take the ulcer."

"No. You don't mean that. You're talking about a child—a new little person coming into the world." Jenni stroked her own rounded belly.

Tears filled Hannah's eyes. "But my world is different from yours. Yours is filled with promise. Mine leaves a lot to be desired. I don't have a husband, and I'm raising JJ on my own. I don't want to get public assistance to raise my children, but I can't earn enough money to—"

"With God all things are possible, Hannah. And what about the baby's father?" She glanced away, then looked back, her head tilted with question. "It's Andrew?"

"Andrew!" Hannah sucked in his name, startled by Jenni's assumption. Yet humiliation charged through her at the thought of admitting the baby was Jack's. "Andrew's not the father, Jenni. Please don't ask. I don't want to talk about it."

Jenni's eyes widened, then the frown returned as if she wasn't certain if Hannah had told the truth. "It's your business, Hannah, but the father deserves to know. And to take responsibility."

Hannah could no longer contain her tears. They ran down her face, and she grasped a nearby towel and held it over her eyes while she wept.

Jenni's gentle touch and soft voice washed over her, and when the words settled in, Hannah realized she'd been praying for her.

Prayer. Sometimes it seemed so hopeless. Hannah had talked with God. She'd turned to Him in her distress, but He seemed to turn His back. How could she explain that she'd kept the rape hidden from everyone? Why had she protected Jack from the abuse he'd submitted her to? Jack deserved nothing.

That wasn't the only reason, she admitted to herself. She wasn't just protecting Jack, but she was hiding her own vulnerability, hiding her shame and violation. She wanted no one's pity. She wanted to stand on her own, to be proud of what she could do for herself and her son.

The pungent smell of chocolate filled the air, and Jenni stepped away and darted to the stove.

Hannah gave a final swipe of the towel and lowered her hand. "I'm sorry. Is it ruined?"

"I think so." She pulled the pot off the burner as the scent of scorched chocolate drifted from it. "Don't worry about it. The chocolate is the least of your problems. Go wash your face, and we won't talk anymore about this now. Just remember that you're in my prayers, and whether it seems so or not, the Lord keeps His promises. Whatever we endure, I believe God is giving us another chance to perfect ourselves in Him."

Hannah shook her head unable to comprehend what Jenni was saying. How could she perfect herself when she seemed to be falling apart?

"And this is the last thing I'll say," Jenni said, pausing with the chocolate-coated spoon pointing toward Hannah. "You should talk to a pastor. Your wellbeing is the most important thing right now. Just think about it."

As Jenni's words soaked into her hardened thoughts, Hannah pulled herself together, relieved that she had finally told someone about the baby *Baby*. The word spread through her. A sweet child. A little boy or girl she could raise without Jack's horrible influence. *Jack.* The name jogged her memory. "Jack's trial is coming up, and I'll probably have to appear."

"Maybe they'll hold him longer this time."

"The lawyer told me that in Michigan, not complying with a protection order is called criminal contempt. He should get at least three months." Her heart skipped. "I hope so, anyway."

Hannah let the topic slide and turned to her work. As she discarded the burnt chocolate, her thoughts shifted to JJ. He'd always been a good boy even though he'd witnessed so many things a child shouldn't see. She'd protected him the best she could, but sometimes she felt alone and afraid. Her courage waned and her strength faded when dealing with Jack. He would be in her life forever, unless...

Jenni's words came into her mind—the Lord keeps His promises. With God anything is possible. JJ's "fruits" popped into Hannah's thoughts, making her smile. She pictured the yellow paper banana with the word *peace* written in bold letters—a peace that passes all understanding. That was God's promise. Hannah let a prayer rise as she worked. *Lord, give me that kind of peace. Give me faith that doesn't weaken in stress. Give me hope because mine has faded.* The telephone's ring jarred her from her reflections, and she glanced up to see Jenni beckoning her. "It's for you."

"Me?" She pressed her index finger into her chest.

"Yes, it's Andrew."

Hannah pulled off her plastic gloves and grasped the receiver, more than surprised to hear Andrew's voice on the line. "I'm sorry to call you at work, Hannah, but I can't sleep, thinking about you. I'm going crazy here and we need to talk. Please."

Andrew's words rang in her ears. Her heart had already softened. She'd known Andrew's crusade was only to help her, but she still didn't like it. But she'd missed him the past week and hadn't slept well, either. "We can't talk now."

"I know. Could I see you tonight? I thought maybe dinner, and then we'll pick up JJ and visit Jemma. She's so much better, and I thought you'd like to see little Philip Junior."

"Philip Junior. So that's what they named him."

"My brother figured it was his last chance for a namesake."

Her chuckle relieved her stress. "I'd love to go. I'll see you tonight." Hannah hung up the phone, still hearing Andrew's excited voice. He loved children. He'd shown that with JJ, but new questions hung in her mind. How could she tell him about her pregnancy? And how would he react?

Chapter Ten

"He's beautiful," Hannah said, leaning over the baby's bassinet. "What do you think, JJ?"

The child tiptoed to get closer. "He's small."

"He sure is," Hannah said. "You were that small once."

JJ looked at her questioningly, then lifted one of the baby's fingers and stared at it before comparing its size to his own.

Jemma chuckled. "The baby looks like Philip, don't you think?"

Hannah gazed at the newborn and then at Jemma. "He has your eyes, I think. Either way, he'll be a handsome young man."

Jemma nodded. "I'm so grateful for this blessing."

With a mother's love, Hannah pressed her hand against her belly. A blessing lived inside of her, but she hadn't accepted it with joy. Questions still rolled around in her mind. What would she do? Would her meager insurance cover the expense? How would she work and pay for childcare? JJ would begin kindergarten in September, and she'd had the wonderful hope of having a little extra income for their needs. Now, a baby.

JJ's interest soon waned, and he skipped from the room, his voice ringing as he told Andrew about seeing the newborn.

Jemma gave Hannah a serious look. "Is something wrong?"

Hannah lifted her head and let her hand slip from its resting place. "I'm fine. I'm just thinking about all you've been through."

"But look," Jemma said, gesturing toward the baby. "He's worth every minute of it."

Hannah made no comment but gazed at the lovely child.

Jemma leaned over and snapped off the yellow duck table lamp. A small night-light glowed near the door, and Hannah headed for the doorway while Jemma gave a final look at her son before following her.

When Hannah stepped into the living room, she saw JJ playing by the toy box with Ellie. As she approached the group around the fireplace, Philip rose. "What do you think of my boy?"

"He's handsome as can be," she said, wondering if Philip also agreed that it had been worth nearly losing his wife for the new baby.

As if hearing her question, Philip motioned for her to be seated, and when she did, he sat, too, then folded his hands between his legs and shook his head. "You know for a fleeting moment, I asked God why He'd given us the joy of a son but threatened to take the child's mother—my wife—but in a moment, I calmed, reassured by the Lord's promises."

"What do you mean?" Hannah asked, unable to believe a man would feel calm in the midst of possibly losing his wife.

"Here," he said, lifting a Bible from the lamp table beside him. "I've kept it right here. I marked the scripture, because the words struck me as I sat there so disheartened and angry. Can you believe? I was so angry at God."

Thinking of her own situation, Hannah could believe it.

Andrew shifted on the sofa beside Hannah and slid his arm across the back cushion. "We've all been there, Philip. Even when we cause our own pain, we blame God."

"I suppose," he said, then lowered his gaze to the Bible. "But these verses came to me as if someone spoke them. They're from Romans 28." He lowered his gaze and read, "'And the Holy Spirit helps us in our distress. For we don't even know what we should pray for, nor how we should pray. But the Holy Spirit prays for us with groanings that cannot be expressed in words. And the Father who knows all hearts knows what the Spirit is saying, for the Spirit pleads for us believers in harmony with God's own will. And we know that God causes everything to work together for the good of those who love God and are called according to his purpose for them.'"

Philip lifted his head as his gaze settled for a moment on each of them. "Do you see what I mean?"

God causes everything to work together for the good of those who love God. The words washed over Hannah. She needed to believe that promise with all her heart. She lowered her hand, feeling the rounding flesh and knowing her body was giving life to a new creation. Warmth spread through her and a renewed sense of determination.

She glanced at JJ still occupied with Ellie and the blocks. Pride filled her. Her son had turned out to be a loving, wonderful child. Why did she worry? She'd struggled most of her life. This new challenge wouldn't be that different, and instead of sorrow, she would have joy, a baby to love and to nurture.

She eyed Jemma's pale face, recalling what she'd gone through to bring her child into the world. Hannah's problems seemed like nothing in the vast scheme of things. *Lord, give me courage and help me to take the challenge. This child is Your plan. Let me be the best I can be, and whatever happens, Lord, I know You'll be by my side.*

The conversation floated past her while plans settled into her head. She needed to attend church regularly. She'd been strong and faith-filled years ago. God hadn't abandoned her. She'd abandoned God. Today she would come home just as Andrew had returned to Loving—humble and anxious, but home.

"Are we there yet?" JJ asked, trying to lean over the car seat but restricted by the seat belt.

Andrew laughed. "I guess that's the typical question, isn't it?"

"Unending," Hannah said. She glanced behind her. "Only a few more minutes."

"I'm glad you agreed to come to Philip's party. He does this every Fourth of July for the employees."

"What happens with the resort guests? Bay Breeze must be busy over the holiday."

"It is, but Philip holds it on the grounds so the working staff can enjoy some of the festivities. Anyway, the resort has plenty of room." He studied her a moment. "Haven't you ever been to Bay Breeze?"

"Never. I know it's along Harbor Drive but I've never had a reason to come down this far. I usually only go as far as the park."

"The grounds are large. The resort has a golf course and tennis courts. You'll enjoy it. And then tonight is the fireworks."

"I should have JJ home by then."

"No need to worry. Jemma's leaving with the children so she agreed to take JJ home with her. I hope you don't mind that I asked."

To Andrew's pleasure, Hannah's expression reflected her acceptance. "Thanks. I usually miss the fireworks."

"I hoped you'd agree." He'd made those plans with apprehension. In the days since they had visited Philip and Jemma's new baby, he'd realized how fragile Hannah's mood had become. She'd always been determined and wanted to take care of things, but lately, he'd watched her change from one mood to another in a second. He suspected something was going on, but so far he didn't know what, and he'd stopped himself from asking Jenni. He figured if anyone did, she would know what was up.

"I'm glad I saw you in church," Hannah said, "I knew you were upset with me, and—"

"*You* were upset with *me*, Hannah. I was confused."

She gave him a repentant look. "I know. It's hard to explain. You do things out of kindness, but it's difficult for me to accept that without thinking you have an ulterior motive."

The word *motive* triggered Andrew's discomfort. He'd realized that his initial charitable motivation had eased into something far deeper and more meaningful. What had once been his attempt to redeem himself with the Lord had now become something far more personal. He couldn't go an hour without thinking of Hannah and JJ. Today as he gazed at her, he longed to run his fingers through the length of her wavy hair and press his mouth against her supple, well-formed lips. The image sent his stomach into a cartwheel.

"I'd like to clear the air today if we can find some quiet time," Andrew said, longing to slip his hand over hers. "What do you say?" Her shy look bounded through his chest.

"I think it's time."

"Good." He smiled at her winsome gaze, then concentrated on the drive. JJ wanted to get there, and if he dallied any longer, he'd have one unhappy boy in the back seat.

When they arrived at Bay Breeze, Andrew pointed to the large white tent far back on the property just below the golf course. As they neared, a sign notified guests that it was a private party. Beneath the white canvas, the sun's heat vanished while a pleasant breeze blew past, smelling of the lake and sunshine.

As Andrew moved deeper beneath the shelter, new aromas met him. "That barbecue smells great," he said, steering her toward a table where his sister-in-law sat holding the baby.

"Hi," Jemma said, her smile as warm as the day. "Glad you could come, Hannah." She caught JJ's eye. "How are you?"

"Fine," he said, sidling nearer to gaze at the baby.

Hannah's heart swelled as Jemma lowered the blanket so JJ could see the baby's face.

"He's still small," he said.

Hannah laughed, loving the feeling. "It takes a while

for babies to grow up. It took almost five years for you to grow as big as you are."

JJ seemed to ponder that idea. Soon Ellie found him, and they ran off with the other children.

"May I hold him?" Hannah asked.

"Certainly," Jemma said, lifting the baby upward so Hannah could take him into her arms. She nestled the child against her chest, filled with a new joy. The scent of talcum powder and milk filled her nostrils, sending her on a journey back to five years earlier when she'd held JJ in her arms.

"You look good holding that baby," Andrew said, coming alongside her. "Some women are meant to be mothers."

Hannah's heart jolted, wondering if he'd guessed. She needed to tell him, but she hadn't found the courage. What would he say? What would he think? What would he do? She avoided responding by nuzzling her cheek against the baby's downy head while she drew in the precious newborn scent. Finally, she released the child back to Jemma's care and settled into a chair.

Time passed as people dropped by to chat. She and Andrew enjoyed some of the wonderful dishes, and they watched the children play, but Hannah's mind kept drifting back to Andrew's earlier suggestion that they clear the air. She longed to talk with him, and she needed to tell him about the court proceedings and Jack. She also yearned for the courage to tell him about her pregnancy.

Finally Andrew took her hand and drew her from the chair. "Will you keep an eye on JJ for us a few minutes?" he asked Jemma. "We want to take a private walk."

"Sure thing," Jemma said, a knowing smile spreading across her face. "Take all the time you need."

Andrew beckoned Hannah toward the sidewalk, and they followed the winding path around the tennis courts and past the outbuildings to the snack bar and pool area of the resort. Breathing in the fragrance of flowers edging the path, she followed him along the sidewalk beside the building and down the hill to the water's edge.

"I hate to ruin a beautiful day, but I need to talk about Jack while we're alone," Hannah began. "I didn't want to talk in front of JJ, but I thought you'd want to know what happened."

"What happened?" Her meaning seemed to register, and Andrew looked at her seriously. "In court."

She nodded. "The judge gave him ninety days and a five-hundred-dollar fine."

"So you have three months reprieve."

"Yes." Her face brightened. "Three whole months to live without worry." She bounced as she took the steps. "So let's not talk about that anymore. Today, let's celebrate."

He seemed to understand and squeezed her hand.

At the bottom of the incline, they stopped, and Hannah drank in the fresh breeze from Lake Michigan, the unique aroma of water, wet sand and fish hidden in the depths of the great lake. "It's beautiful," she said, gazing at the diamond-studded whitecaps that rolled to shore.

"So are you," Andrew said.

His comment jarred her—so unexpected, so foreign. She arched a brow, wondering where the comment had come from. "Thanks, but I—"

His smile faded. "I know you're surprised, but I mean it." He linked her arm in his and guided her onto the boardwalk that followed the beach to the lighthouse pier.

"I need you to explain things," Hannah said after struggling with what had just happened. "We've become friends. I've understood that to a degree, but not totally. You're so out of my league, Andrew."

"Out of your league. What does that mean? I told you I'm not even in the minor leagues if you compare me to Philip. Don't you understand?"

His serious expression made her realize that maybe she didn't. "I know you left home to make your own way. When you didn't succeed, you came back, feeling humbled and disappointed in yourself."

"It's deeper than that. I fell into an abyss, a hole so deep I saw hell."

Hell? The tremor in his voice captured her attention, and for the first time, she understood how deeply he'd suffered from his past mistakes. "No matter what you did, you grew up with that silver spoon they talk about. You have an education. You came from a family that knows which fork and knife to use at a fancy dinner."

"Do you think forks and knives or silver spoons are what's important in life?"

His despairing tone turned bitter. She stopped and touched his arm. "I'm not making light of your problems, Andrew. I'm sure those years were difficult. You found yourself in a lifestyle you'd never known before."

"I found myself in iniquity. I drank too much. I lied and sometimes cheated. I toyed with sexual favors on the pretense I was someone important. I threw my father's hard-earned money away on sin. I'm poor, Hannah. I have nothing to call my own."

"But look around you—" She gestured toward the expanse of the resort. Her hand trembled, hearing his confession.

"This belongs to Philip. I work for my brother. I'm salaried like any employee here. I explained that."

Hannah had felt no reaction to Andrew calling himself poor. He seemed far richer than she had ever been. He had a steady job, a nice home, an education. "Are you happy?"

"I'm happy to be home. I'm happy to have met you and JJ. I'm content."

"Then that's all that counts. What more could you want?"

A new look edged across Andrew's face. "I want forgiveness."

Forgiveness? "But you have that. You told me about the party—the fatted calf, remember?"

"Philip forgave me. My father even forgave me, and I try to convince myself that God has forgiven me, but I haven't forgiven myself for the hurt I caused my family."

She stopped and gazed into his eyes, aware of the pain that exuded from his words and reflected in his expression. "You know I've struggled with my faith, too, but I've never forgotten that God can look into our hearts. He sees our repentance and our sorrow. Jesus died to forgive our sins. They're wiped clean, making us as pure as baby Philip Junior. You have to believe that."

His eyes looked deeply into hers, but he didn't respond.

"Do you remember yesterday during the sermon when pastor read the lessons?" she said, praying he would understand. "One really struck me, and I reread it when I got home. It was from Second Corinthians. I have it bookmarked at home so I can read it each day. It says something about God's grace being all we need. That we should rejoice in our weakness—our hardships, persecutions and trials—because then we're drawn closer to the Lord, and we become stronger because Jesus is our strength. Think about it, Andrew. Your trials have made you a better person through Jesus."

Andrew shook his head. "I guess I wasn't listening yesterday. I had to hit the depths of despair before I finally pleaded with God to lift me up."

"And He'd been just waiting for you to call on Him again." Hannah felt amazed that God had given her the words and the strength to say them.

The sun slipped behind a cloud, and a cool breeze blew off the water. A chill shivered down her back.

Andrew drew closer and slipped his arm around her shoulders. "This leads me to what I wanted to talk about."

The heat from his body radiated through her. Yet his statement made her uneasy. What else would he drop on her? "Aren't we talking about it now, Andrew?"

His gaze softened as he drew her more fully into his arms. "Only part of it. I wanted you to know the truth before I tell you how I feel."

How I feel. Hannah held her breath. This is what she'd longed to know, and today she would have her answer.

"You said we're friends, and we are, but Hannah, I'm feeling more than friendship. I can't get you or JJ out of my mind. You fill my thoughts and dreams."

"Andrew, if you're—"

"Wait. Let me finish before you say anything. It's taken a lot of courage to say this."

She closed her eyes a moment to steady herself.

"I have nothing to offer you. Yes, I have a job and a house, but my life savings have been wasted. My feelings have grown beyond friendship. I'd like the opportunity to date you with the idea that—"

"Andrew do you know what you're asking?" A thrill coupled with dread filled her at his admission, and her hand slid to her belly, knowing another child was grow-

ing there, a child Andrew might resent, a child she'd
been unable to tell him about. "I have a ready-made
family. I have an ex-husband who wants to destroy me.
What do I have to offer you but more heartache and
problems?"

He drew her to his chest. "You and JJ are worth more
to me than I can tell you. I can handle problems, but I
can't handle being without you."

The fragrance of his aftershave washed over her, and
she breathed in the scent, longing to put away her fears,
but still she couldn't help questioning whether she was
Andrew's atoning mission, a way to earn forgiveness, a
sacrifice for his sins.

"I'm not asking you for a commitment, Hannah,"
Andrew said, breaking into her muddied thoughts. "I
just wanted to let you know how I feel about you."

She found the courage to raise her eyes to his, and
there she saw a gentleness that made her weak. "I care
about you, too, Andrew, more than I can say, but I've
been through so much. I don't want to make promises
I can't keep. My life has been a mess and it still is, more
than you know." *Dear God give me the courage to tell
him.* "I—"

"I'm asking for us to spend time together. I want to
hold you in my arms." His grasp tightened around her
until she felt his heart beating against hers. "I want to
kiss you."

Her heart thundered. She felt her lids droop and close
as his mouth touched hers. Gentle, warm pleasure rolled
over her as her pulse quickened and her heart danced.
It had been so long since she'd been touched with such
tenderness, when soft lips had touched hers, sending her
head spinning.

A tremor rolled through her, and Andrew eased back, his gaze riveted to hers. "This kiss is worth more than money, more than success."

Hannah couldn't find words to respond. If she admitted her feelings, she would have to tell him about the child and ruin the lovely moment still vibrating through her.

"If you understand what you're in for, I'd love to spend time with you," she whispered, longing for his mouth to capture hers again.

He seemed to hear her thoughts. His fingers wove through her hair, cupping her head against his palm, and his lips sought hers, the kiss deeper and longer, sending her on a journey to the sky.

Chapter Eleven

Andrew sat in his car outside the candy store, his mind racing. He and Hannah had spent the past month together as he'd dreamed. They'd walked the beach, spent time at the park with JJ, sat together on Sunday mornings in church, enjoyed visits with friends and with Philip's family, but today he feared things were about to change.

Something had happened. He sensed it. Hannah had become quieter, her kisses not as yielding, her face masked by an unknown element that set him on edge.

He'd reviewed their time together, looking for something he'd done to offend her or something about their relationship that put a barrier between them. He could think of nothing.

The sedan engine purred while the air conditioner sent a whooshing sound from the vents, circulating cool air to diminish the August heat. Even in the cooler car, beads of perspiration dotted his hairline and above his lip. He wiped them away, wondering if it was the sun or his edginess making them appear.

Garnering courage, he turned off the ignition and opened the car door. The summer sun's rays engulfed him as he stepped onto the concrete. He gave the door a push and hit the lock button, then turned and gazed at Loving Chocolate.

Jenni's store had grown since its opening. The front window displayed candy boxes decorated in seasonal packaging. Today, large gold-colored bows held silk roses or daisies—and boxes of every size. Multi-colored bags of coffee beans had been placed in one corner of the window with a table set with fancy cups and saucers and a dish of cookies. Jenni and Todd had good business sense, something he envied.

Andrew prayed he could catch Jenni alone for a moment without alerting Hannah to the fact that he was there. If anyone knew Hannah's problem, Andrew figured Jenni would. He tugged at the handle, and a bell tinkled as he stepped inside.

Cool air washed over him along with the scent of fresh ground coffee and rich chocolate. Jenni's head bobbed up from behind the counter. "Hi," she said with a look of curiosity. "You usually come in the back." Her arm swung toward the kitchen door.

He held a finger against his lips. "I wanted to talk with you alone." He glanced toward the kitchen, praying Hannah hadn't heard his voice.

Jenni shifted from behind the display case and came around the counter, a frown spreading across her face. "Is something wrong, Andrew?"

"I just need your input."

Her frown changed to a look of anticipation, and she waved him toward the coffee brewer. "Have a cup. I can sit with you a minute until a customer comes in."

He grabbed a chocolate-colored mug with the store's logo imprinted on it and poured the coffee, then took a seat at a small round table where Jenni had just settled.

"I hope this is good news?" she said, her voice not as convincing as her words.

"It's nothing like that." He saw her grimace. "Not yet anyway, but I'm worried about Hannah. Something's wrong, Jenni. We decided to see where things would lead us, but I sense her pulling away. What have I done? What's wrong? If anyone would know, you would."

Jenni's gaze lowered to the table, a frown spreading across her face again. "Don't ask me Hannah's business, Andrew, please. You need to talk with her. She cares about you very much. I know that."

"Then what is it?"

"Are you listening? I'm not going to answer questions that Hannah needs to answer for you."

She gave him a questioning look as if he should know what was wrong. He felt his shoulders sag. Maybe he should know, but he didn't. He didn't understand women any better than his business ventures.

Disappointment grew when Jenni rose from the chair and returned to the counter. He'd counted on her, and she'd let him down. He swallowed the last of the coffee before rising. "Is Hannah in the back?"

Jenni nodded. "You can go inside." She gestured toward the employee door to the kitchen.

After talking with her, he felt more confused than when he'd come into the shop, and, despite a warning within that he shouldn't force Hannah to talk, he followed Jenni's invitation and pushed open the door.

"What are you doing here?" Hannah said when he stepped into the kitchen.

"Coming to see you."

"But you usually—" She motioned toward the back door.

He captured her arm and drew her closer. His lips touched hers, and she returned the kiss until that same barrier stopped her.

"Is something wrong?" she asked brusquely, pulling away.

His gaze captured hers, and he wanted to tell her that was the question he planned to ask her, but he knew he had to ease into it. They needed to talk, and he scuffled for a logical explanation for his visit. "Nothing's wrong with me. I was just passing and wondered if…" He grasped for an idea. "…if you'd like to go to the Coast Guard Craft Fair tonight at the park in Grand Haven." He lifted his shoulders, thankful he'd recalled reading about it in the morning paper.

"Craft fair? What about JJ? He'd be bored."

"But you wouldn't be. Let's see if we can find a sitter."

She focused on the melting chocolate and stirred the large pot before turning her attention back to his offer. "All right. I'll get a sitter."

Her quick smile lifted Andrew's spirit. Maybe it was only his imagination, but his gut told him they had a problem.

Hannah held the package while Andrew dug into his wallet for the cash. "Thanks for buying JJ the wooden train. He'll love it."

"I always wanted one of those when I was a kid, and my dad got me a real Lionel set with all the tracks and a village."

Looking at the expression on his face, she couldn't

help but grin. "Poor child. Most kids would give up the rest of their toys for a train with tracks and a village."

"I was different."

"I guess," she said, trying to sound lighthearted, but her mind kept coming back to their differences. He might have wanted a wooden train, but his father had the wherewithal to buy him something even better. Andrew seemed destined for better things than Hannah could offer him.

"Want to sit and listen to the music awhile?" he asked, motioning toward the country tune drifting across the park.

She nodded and turned in that direction, sensing Andrew had more on his mind than music. He wove his fingers through hers as they passed the fountain and headed toward the band.

Tents dotted the lawn where stained glass, hand-crafted jewelry, quilts and fancy pillows were displayed. Near the trio Andrew guided her to an empty bench, and she sat, trying to focus on the activities around her rather than on the thoughts running through her mind. She set the packages on the bench and rested her tense back against the slats.

Andrew drew her closer and kissed her hair. "Would you like something cold to drink?"

She started to answer, but instead said what had been on her mind. "What I really want is to know what's on your mind. Something's bothering you, Andrew. I know you well enough to spot it in your behavior."

"I guess I'm not very subtle."

She saw his jaw tighten while apprehension filled her. She'd hidden her secret too long, and now she feared someone had suspected and told him. "Is this about me?"

"Yes."

"Did someone tell you something about me?"

His eyes narrowed as a frown settled on his face. "No, but I wish you would."

She nodded as relief washed over her. *Thank you, Lord. I know I have to tell him even if it ends our relationship. I can't put it off. Dear Father, give me the courage to say it right so he'll understand.*

She lifted her eyes to Andrew's and witnessed a depth of sadness that startled her. What had he been thinking?

"This has to do with us?" he said, more a question than a statement.

She shook her head. "In a roundabout way."

His frown deepened while she struggled for the words. "I don't know how to tell you, Andrew, and I can't believe you haven't noticed already." Her hand slid to the growing bulge she'd tried to cover with loose-fitting tops.

"Noticed? What is it? Don't play games. Just tell me."

"This isn't a game. It's difficult for me to talk about it. I've been distraught over the situation, and I'm trying to accept it and be happy."

"Please, Hannah, get on with it." His eyes burned with questions.

She drew in a breath and forced the words into the air. "I'm pregnant."

His back straightened like a puppet jerked on a string. "You're what?"

The look in his eyes—disbelief, disappointment, shock—broke her heart. "I'm pregnant. I'm expecting a baby."

"A baby?" He glanced at her abdomen, then looked at her with disbelief. "I don't understand."

What more could she say? "There's nothing to understand. I'm expecting a child. It's due in mid December."

"Mid December? How long have you known this?"

"I saw the doctor over two months ago. At first, I'd thought it was stress. I couldn't believe the truth."

He didn't respond but stared at her while his face twisted with emotion. "I don't understand how…" He waved his hands in the air. "You should have told me."

"I was afraid."

His head jerked around to face her. "Afraid of what?"

"Of this," she said, gesturing to him. "Of how you'd react. I care for you, Andrew. You've been wonderful to us, and I—"

He stood and leaned over, his face inches from hers. "I don't understand, Hannah. You mean you and Jack—"

"It's not like that at all."

His arms dropped to his sides. "Then what is it?" He caved onto the bench.

"The baby is J—" She couldn't say the name. Her stomach churned as tears welled in her eyes. "It doesn't matter." She rose. "Please take me home. Or should I call a cab?"

"It's Jack." Disgust filled his voice, but he didn't move. Appearing frozen to the spot, he peered at her as if deciding which to do. "Explain to me how this happened?"

His words struck her like a knife. "Use your head, Andrew. What do you think?" She clenched her teeth, aching with regret. Andrew didn't want to hear the truth, and she wouldn't grovel to ask for forgiveness. She'd done nothing. If he couldn't figure that out, then he could stand there with his mouth hanging open forever. She didn't care.

"Thanks for the lovely evening." She let the sarcasm

pierce him, then grasped the packages she'd purchased and sped across the lawn toward the sidewalk.

"Hannah!"

She refused to slow her steps or even glance over her shoulder. Andrew had demoralized her. What did he think? Did he think she would give herself to Jack voluntarily?

As she charged away, her foot sank into a rut and her ankle twisted, but the pain that shot through her leg could not compare to the stabbing ache that tore at her heart. With determination, she yanked her foot free and kept walking.

Andrew watched Hannah dash toward the street, and a moment passed before he came to his senses. He grabbed the package she'd left on the bench—the wooden train—and bolted after her. "Hannah!"

She ignored his cry and hurried ahead.

He stopped calling and used his energy to run after her, doubling his efforts when he saw her stumble. When he reached her, his chest ached from the exertion and from the shock of having her walk away without an explanation. "Please, don't leave without resolving this, Hannah. Please."

She turned to face him while tears rolled down her cheeks. "I can't talk about this now. Please. If you have any respect at all—any mercy—just take me home."

He helped her to the sedan in silence while his mind struggled with what to say, what to do. He was in agony as he relived how a pleasant evening had turned into a nightmare. What had she expected? Had she thought he would be joyful to hear she'd been sleeping with her ex-husband?

Carla's comment the day he picked up Hannah's belongings had set him on edge. Today the words blared in his head. She'd mentioned Jack had left Hannah's apartment about three in the morning. He'd asked himself why Jack had stayed so long. Now it made sense. Hannah had sneaked out after Jack had fallen asleep.

They'd been in bed together. The image sickened him.

Horrible thoughts charged across his mind, and, not wanting to say anything he'd regret, he clamped his teeth together until they ached. The silence stressed him, and when they reached Loving Treasures, Andrew still had nothing to say.

"I'll get out here," Hannah said as he turned into the driveway at the side of her apartment. Before he could tell her he'd pull closer to the entrance, she'd opened the door and gingerly stepped out, slamming the door without a goodbye.

He sat staring at her, wondering what to do and what to think. The dusky sky had grown darker, and Andrew turned on his headlights as he backed into the street and pulled away, his heart heavy and his mind burdened with Hannah's confession. Pregnant with Jack's baby.

Pregnant. Confusion rolled through him, then envy. He'd been dreaming of the day he and Hannah might marry. JJ would be his little boy, and he'd hoped, prayed, that he and Hannah would have a child of their own. Two children. Even more.

His gut ached as he continued down Washington Street. Ahead he saw the shelter where he'd taken Hannah that first night. He'd felt sorry for her, a woman abused and broken. Suddenly the truth struck him. How could he have been so dense? Hannah wouldn't give herself to Jack. He must have forced her—violated her and beaten her. Or... Speculation wouldn't offer the answer. Only Hannah could tell him the truth, and now he'd angered her with his lack of sensitivity, and he didn't blame her.

As he drew closer to the shelter, next door he noticed Ken Dewitt and his kids outside their house. He hesitated, longing to consult someone wiser than he'd been. Instead, he pushed on the gas pedal. Then at the last minute his foot shifted to the brake.

Ken lifted his hand in greeting.

Almost without control, Andrew pulled to the curb and stopped.

Ken seemed to be waiting for him and grinned as Andrew pushed open his door and stepped into the street.

"I'm babysitting," he called, holding Dillon on his arm and Gracelynne at his side. "Glad you stopped by."

Babysitting. The word sent his thoughts back to Hannah, and his gut ached again. Why had he stopped? "I'm just passing by. I dropped Hannah at home." He realized he couldn't tell Ken the details of what had happened. How could he explain? How could he divulge Hannah's startling news?

"Out for dinner?" Ken asked.

"We went to the Coast Guard Craft Fair at the park."

Ken chuckled. "Did you see Annie?"

"No."

"She's helping one of the church ladies at her booth. You know women. They love shopping."

Andrew tried to smile, but his face felt as if it would crack.

Ken's expression shifted to concern. "Something wrong?"

Andrew shook his head, irritated that he couldn't

keep the stress from his face. "A little misunderstanding that's all." He brushed away his response.

"Amazing how a few words can ruin a nice evening."

His comment caught Andrew by surprise. "You and Annie argue much?"

"Not often, but sometimes we butt heads." He beckoned Andrew toward the house. "Come in and have a drink. I can make coffee, or we have pop."

Now that he'd stopped, Andrew wanted to escape, but Ken seemed so pleased to see him, how could he leave?

He followed Ken and the kids up the steps, noticing the homey porch swing. He would prefer to sit there in the gloom rather than have Ken see his face in the light, but Ken opened the front door, and Andrew could do nothing but follow.

"Have a seat. I need to get Dillon into his crib and Gracelynne ready for bed. I'll just a minute."

Andrew settled into a chair, his mind rushing like a brush fire trying to figure out how to get out of the situation he'd gotten himself into with Ken while pondering what had happened between him and Hannah.

Why didn't Hannah realize that hearing about her pregnancy would throw him off balance? His thoughts billowed like the Lake Michigan waves, trying to imagine why Hannah would allow an abusive man, no longer her husband, into her house.

The vision struck him. She hadn't. That was obvious. Jack had forced his way in, just as he had forced himself on her.

Anger bristled up his spine as he pictured the burden Hannah had carried alone. Why hadn't she just told him from the beginning? Why hadn't she told the police that Jack had sexually assaulted her? He leaned back against the chair, his thoughts raging like a stormy sea.

Ken's voice traveled from the distant bedroom as he talked with Gracelynne. He heard Ken's goodnight, then footsteps.

"How about that drink now? Sorry, but if Annie came home and the kids weren't in bed, then you'd see some head-butting." He grinned and motioned toward the kitchen. "Cold or hot?"

"A cola is fine. Thanks."

Ken vanished through the doorway while Andrew drew in a calming breath. He tried to sort through his re-action to Hannah. Anger. No, he felt rejected. Andrew's shoulders ached with the knotted emotions. He'd learned to harden himself to hurt. Or he thought he had. Had getting involved with Hannah been a horrible mistake?

Emptiness shot through his chest. What would life be like without Hannah now that he'd found her? If she'd only explained. If Jack had done the unthinkable, why hadn't she confessed, and—

Confessed? She would have been the victim. Why would she confess? She would have been mortified, vandalized, violated. His hands trembled when he raised them to his jaw, and Andrew longed to leave, to forget facing Ken while his thoughts were in such upheaval.

"Here you go," Ken said, striding into the room holding a glass with ice and cola.

"Thanks," Andrew said accepting the glass and taking a lengthy swallow. His dry mouth welcomed the drink.

"So you and Hannah had an argument. Don't let it weigh on you. One thing I've learned is love is far more valuable than gold. It's worth fighting for."

"This problem is complex, and I've hurt Hannah with

my reaction." Andrew winced as he realized he'd opened his mouth and said too much.

"Nothing is too complex for the Lord. I'm listening if you want to talk about it."

Chapter Twelve

The last thing Andrew wanted to do was talk about what had happened with Hannah, yet if he truly believed in God's promises, nothing was too big for the Lord. He'd left God out of the picture.

He leaned forward, his hands folded, elbows resting on his knees, and stared at the floor. What could he say? What could he reveal? He wondered if Annie knew about the pregnancy and had already told Ken, but he couldn't take the chance.

Andrew's shoulders raised as he gathered courage. "I know God can move mountains and part seas, but I doubt if dealing with my confusion is important."

Ken's eyebrows raised. "God counts the hairs on your head. Wouldn't he care even more about what's in your heart and mind?"

"It's just that we're human. We make stupid mistakes and say stupid things. It's nothing, really."

"It's up to you, Andrew. I don't want to pry."

"I know you're trying to be helpful. I'm not like you, Ken. I was a strong Christian once, but I slipped, and even now I forget to act like the Christian I say I am. Someone like you who's been close to the Lord all your life, you—"

"Hold on." Ken raised his hand like a traffic cop. "You're wrong. I'm a new Christian, Andrew. My past doesn't win a prize, either. I've made horrible mistakes, and Annie's faith is what helped me to understand how full life can be when we let Jesus carry our load."

Andrew's chest tightened, looking at Ken's serious expression. Feelings. He hated them sometimes. Emotions. They were a woman's MO, not a man's. Yet feelings had taken hold of his life. "I wish I was more like you, Ken. You always seem confident in your faith. Annie's mentioned you attend Bible study and go to church every Sunday. I figure—"

"You figured wrong. I had a troubled childhood. My dad's view of scripture was that discipline meant a punch in the face. My past is a mess. I got into serious trouble when I was a teenager. None of us is perfect."

His face paled as he searched Andrew's face. "I sense the Lord wants me to tell you this, but it's still hard to talk about even today." Ken released a ragged sigh that reached Andrew. "I served a prison sentence for breaking and entering along with destruction of property. I lived with that guilt and fear of people finding out, Andrew, until I finally had the courage to tell Annie before I asked her to marry me. I became a stronger Christian through Annie's efforts. I don't like to talk about the past, but I know I'm forgiven."

Ken's confession fell on Andrew like a barbell while his own past added a hundred pounds to the pressure. "You've shocked me, Ken. You've always seemed the epitome of a devout Christian, so free from sinful ways."

"Free from sin? I don't know anyone who is."

"You know what I mean. You always say and do the right thing." Andrew shook his head, then took another swig of the soft drink, hoping to compose himself. "I guess that's my error, basing conclusions on guesses."

"Let's get back to you and Hannah for a minute," Ken said. "Annie thinks a lot of Hannah. I know Hannah's been through a bad time, too. She deserves every chance for a good life."

Fighting the lump in his throat, Andrew only nodded.

Ken continued. "One thing I've learned since having a personal relationship with the Lord is in Proverbs 3. 'Trust in the Lord with all your heart and lean not on your own understanding; in all your ways acknowledge him, and he will make your paths straight.' In other words, lean on God and not your frustration. That's the best lesson I've learned."

"Good point. I've tried to reason things out on my own, but that didn't work. I made a real blunder with Hannah."

"It's easy to do. Even though we're Christians, you said it yourself, we're human. We sin, but that's what's so neat about God. He understands that and gives us a chance to learn and fix it."

Andrew already knew everything Ken had said, but today it made more sense. Now he needed to decide how to make things right.

"There's another verse from Proverbs that's guided my married life. It's so important to me I've memorized it. 'By wisdom a house is built, and through understanding it is established; through knowledge its rooms are filled with rare and beautiful treasures.'" He swung his arm toward the hallway. "I just tucked two of those rare and beautiful treasures into bed. The other one will be home soon. Nothing is more valuable than family."

Andrew's chest stung with grief, recalling what he'd done to his father and brother. The day Philip had wept in his arms filled Andrew's mind. He'd said it himself. Nothing is more valuable than family. God had forgiven him. Letting go of the past made all the difference.

"And one more thought, then I'll shut up."

Andrew chuckled, glad that Ken hadn't kept quiet.

"Memorize this verse, and it can save a relationship or a marriage. Ephesians 4:26. 'In your anger do not sin. Do not let the sun go down while you are still angry.' Annie and I have agreed that we don't go to bed until we've resolved a conflict. We never part company without talking over a problem. It saves both of us from heartache. If a relationship is worth keeping, it's worth the effort to understand, to resolve and to forgive."

Andrew couldn't respond. He let Ken's words soak in and sensed the Lord had directed him here to learn the wisdom he'd longed to hear.

"Thanks," he said, finally. "I know what I have to do. I'll talk with Hannah tonight."

After the sitter left, Hannah put JJ to bed and sank onto the sofa. She curled her legs beneath her and rested her head against the cushion, thinking about her earlier confrontation with Andrew. Her world had crumbled in the blink of an eye. Hearing Andrew's harsh words, she'd been barraged with confusion. She'd feared he would take the news badly, and he had. But being correct disappointed her. She wanted him to understand, to take her in his arms and tell her everything would be okay.

She'd allowed her naïveté to catch her off guard again. She'd given her heart to a man who really didn't know her. She'd been afraid that might happen again if she fell in love.

And she had fallen in love with every ounce of her being.

She felt numb with the realization. Andrew had walked out of her life. In truth, she'd walked out of his, but for good reason. His reaction had disappointed her beyond words.

Hannah closed her eyes, overwhelmed by fatigue. She'd been let down, embarrassed and upset. She knew better than to go to bed now. She would toss and turn all night until daylight peeked through the crevice between the shade and windowsill. Her head spun until the dizziness overcame her, and she felt herself drifting into an uneasy sleep.

The doorbell jolted Hannah awake. Then a distant rapping sent her heart to her throat while her pulse thumped. Dazed with sleep, she pushed her legs off the sofa and rose, her knees weak from grogginess. She grasped the corner of a chair to gain her balance.

As she approached the door to the staircase, the bell rang again. What time was it? She glanced at the clock and realized it wasn't late. She'd drifted to sleep on the couch. Jack? No, Jack wouldn't ring the bell, she told herself.

Amid her thoughts, she heard her name. She moved closer to the door, unlocked it, then opened it a crack.

She heard the call again.

"Hannah!"

Recognizing Andrew's voice, Hannah opened the apartment door and stood a moment, deciding what to do. She could ignore him or answer the downstairs door. Her hand froze on the knob while the word *forgiveness* rang in her mind.

But why Lord? Why should I take a chance again? The answer rolled over Hannah. Because Andrew had been kind throughout her ordeal. He'd been caring and helpful—too helpful at times—but he'd become her dearest friend. He'd made a mistake with his reaction, but maybe she'd made a mistake, too, by walking away. She had known he'd be startled, but she'd hoped for compassion.

Andrew's rapping sounded up the staircase, and his plaintive voice calling her name drew her to descend the steps. When she stepped to the door, she saw his face in the security light at the side of the building.

The noise stopped as his voice penetrated the barred entry window. "I need to talk with you. Please."

His sad eyes and the contrite look on his face sent Hannah's emotions tumbling. She turned the lock and opened the door.

"Thank you," he said. "May I come in?"

"You'd better, before the police arrest you for disturbing the peace."

"I'm sorry. I was afraid you wouldn't answer."

Seeing him now made her happy she'd relented. Hannah turned and headed up the stairs while Andrew's heavier steps followed hers.

She waved him inside, and he headed through the doorway into the living room. She shut and locked the door, and when she joined him, he crumpled into a chair and dropped his face into his hands. "I'm sorry, Hannah. I know I reacted badly, but you startled me. No, it hurt me. I couldn't think." He raised his gaze to hers.

Hannah had to fight herself from pulling him into her arms. Andrew, the strong comforter, looked like a beaten child, and his appearance set her back. "I shouldn't have walked away, Andrew, but your reaction upset me. I'd hoped you would understand."

"I think I do now, but you didn't explain. I was startled. Confused."

She remained standing, hoping to make him realize the depth of the offense. "You didn't give me time to, but it's really not your problem, Andrew. It's mine."

He rose and walked to her side. "I care about you, Hannah, so it's my problem, too. I was afraid—" He sought her eyes as if unable to say what he had thought.

"You were afraid of what? That I'd willingly slept with him?"

His gaze dropped. "I didn't know what to think."

"Andrew, we've only known each other a few months, but I hope you know me better than that."

He lifted his head. "He forced you?" His response sounded confident as if he knew he was correct.

A knot twisted between her shoulder blades. "Yes." She lifted her hand and pressed it against her chest.

Andrew's eyes darkened, and Hannah could see he was struggling to understand what her *yes* meant.

"He raped you."

"Yes. More than once."

"Dear Lord, no." His voice was weighted with horror. "Did you tell anyone? The police? Anyone?"

She shook her head. "I felt unclean and violated. I didn't know what to do. What anyone could do."

He grasped her shoulders. "I'll tell you what I feel, Hannah. I'm angry. I'm incensed. I want vengeance."

"Vengeance belongs to the Lord, not you or me. What can you do? It happened, but it won't happen again."

Andrew wrapped his arms around her shoulders and

drew her closer. She pressed her head against his chest and felt his heart thumping against hers. When she raised her head, Andrew's gaze caught hers before his lips found her mouth. The gentle kiss blanketed her sadness and warmed the icy thoughts rooted in the back of her mind.

He drew back, and his voice sounded husky. "I'm so sorry. Sorry for what happened and how I reacted."

"I'm sorry for walking away. I should have told you the rest."

"The rest?"

"How it happened."

He nodded. "It's too awful to think about. You've been alone with this."

"To be honest, I told Jenni. I had to talk with someone about the baby."

A look of disappointment charged across his face, and she realized she'd hurt him with her admission.

"I needed to clear my mind, Andrew. My first thoughts were about whether I could love this child when it was conceived in such a brutal way."

His gaze lowered to her abdomen as if trying to envision a baby there. Then he lifted his eyes. "But it's a child."

Though he said the words, Hannah recognized the mixed emotions crossing his face. "My horrible thought was fleeting. I couldn't abandon my child. I'm carrying a little life inside me." Her hand slid to her rounded tummy. "I love this baby already."

Andrew's eyes searched hers. "We'll work it out. I'm with you, Hannah, if you'll have me."

"Why would you want to?"

He embraced her again as he whispered into her hair. "You're as important to me as life itself. You and JJ."

You and JJ. But what about the child growing inside her?

Andrew rose from his desk and looked out his office window toward the back of the resort. He'd been trying to concentrate, but for the past month, he'd been distracted. He wanted to support Hannah and her new child, yet he felt anger and resentment for what had happened.

Hannah wasn't to blame. Logic told him that, but jealousy jabbed at him every time he thought about it. Hannah would have another child, and Andrew feared resenting the new baby. His feelings made no sense, but he knew they were real. He'd come to love JJ, a child already born to Hannah and the madman—he seemed unable to say Jack's name—but facing another child, Andrew's logic left him and bitter emotions took its place.

Emotions were the part of life Andrew wanted to escape. When he'd learned his father had died, Andrew had been tormented by his avoidance of the funeral. He'd lived with his heart in his throat while he watched his family money sink faster than the *Titanic,* and he'd had no idea what to do about it.

Andrew had avoided serious romantic relationships until he'd met Hannah, and then he'd let down his guard. Perhaps his original interest in her had resulted from compassion, but he questioned that. Hannah was a woman who'd been dealt a bad blow, and he admired her strength. He'd felt drawn to her from the moment they met. At first, he'd seen a comrade—someone who understood hard times. Perhaps the look in her eyes had drawn him or her vulnerability had captured his interest. But her determination and fortitude had been what fascinated him.

Now it didn't matter what had caused his involvement with her. His life had become enmeshed with Hannah's, and a plan had developed in his mind. He'd prayed their relationship would grow into something permanent. Yet how could he follow through now with the constant jabs of envy and worry that he would never be able to accept this new life?

Jack had devastated Hannah's life for years. In another month, he would be free to torment her again unless he'd learned his lesson, but Andrew didn't think anything would change Jack. And if he abused drugs and alcohol, Andrew feared what he'd do next.

Andrew bit the edge of a ragged fingernail, a habit he'd acquired since hearing about Hannah's pregnancy. The rough cuticle bugged him, just as the difficult situation did.

"Are you busy?"

Philip's voice jerked Andrew from the window, and he spun around, his arm dropping to his side. "Just taking a break," he said, wishing Philip hadn't caught him staring out the window. "So what brings you here?"

Philip stepped into his office and closed the door. "I wanted to talk with you privately."

Andrew felt his brow wrinkle, and his mouth turn down into a frown. "Did I do something wrong?"

"This isn't about Bay Breeze. You're doing a great job. This is personal."

Personal? Andrew had no idea what had riled Philip, but he saw his stance and knew it was serious. "Would you like to sit?" He motioned toward a chair.

But Philip didn't budge. He stood near the door, his

uneasy look growing more tense. "I need to talk with you about Hannah."

"Hannah?" If his brother had gripes about his relationship with Hannah, Andrew was ready for a fight. "What about her?"

"She's a very nice woman, Andrew. Jemma and I both like her, but I'm concerned…"

Andrew's fingers knotted into fists. "Concerned about what?"

Philip dug his hands into his pockets. "She's pregnant, isn't she?"

His brother's words had caught Andrew off-guard. "How would you—"

"Jemma noticed."

Of course. Women noticed those things, Andrew supposed. He'd barely noticed Hannah's clothes getting tighter, but she'd complained about it recently. The past weeks she'd begun to wear loose-fitting tops to cover the bulge.

Andrew's cheek ticked with his brother's challenge, and a hot flush crept to his face. "Yes, she's pregnant."

Philip's shoulders relaxed, and he ambled forward and clasped Andrew's shoulder. "Don't you think you should talk with the pastor? You want to do the right thing, don't you?"

Do the right thing? The words spun in Andrew's head until the meaning struck him. "It's not what you think." What could he say without breaking Hannah's confidence? "Look, Philip, I appreciate your concern, but this is Hannah's problem and—"

Philips hands dropped from his shoulders as he drew back. "Hannah's problem? I can't believe you'd say that." Disgust filled his face. "When you were younger, I wasn't surprised you acted without thought for the family's reputation or God's will, but you're not a kid any longer. You're a man, and you have to accept responsibilities."

Andrew held up his hand. "Philip, please. Hannah and I are doing what we think is best. Give me credit for knowing the difference between right and wrong."

Even as he said the words, anger seethed through him. His brother thought he was the baby's father. Philip thought so little of him that he had come to that conclusion. Hadn't he realized that Andrew had changed? He'd tried to atone for his sins since he returned. He'd been the epitome of an upstanding citizen.

Philip raised his shoulders, expelling a deep stream of air. "People will talk. You know that."

"Gossip means nothing to me. I've had to deal with that most of my adult life."

"And what about Hannah? How does she feel about people gossiping?" Philip's eyes flickered with irritation. "Don't you want to protect her?"

"That's what I've been trying to do, Philip, but you wouldn't understand. Please give us credit and give us time to sort things out. I'll do the right thing. I'm sorry, but I can't talk about this now."

Philip flung his arms upward at his sides, then turned toward the door. "It's your life. It's your reputation."

It's *your* reputation you're worried about, Philip, Andrew thought. But before he could utter the comeback, his brother opened the door and shot from the office.

Andrew drew in a ragged breath and sank into his chair. His own brother thought the worst. What would others think of Hannah? He didn't care about himself, but Hannah didn't need to be shamed anymore than she already had been.

The truth struck him. He'd done the same thing to Hannah. He'd jumped to conclusions, and he'd presumed things. He lowered his face into his hands and massaged his forehead. *Lord, please give me the answers.*

He placed his hand on the telephone receiver, then hesitated. What good would it do? Why upset her? He'd talk to her later. If Jemma had already noticed Hannah's condition, he could only guess that half the town had, too. They'd be buzzing with gossip.

Chapter Thirteen

Hannah kissed JJ's cheek and turned out his bedroom light. "Love you."

"Love you," he murmured, already drifting to sleep.

She paused a moment outside his door, reviewing what she needed to say to Andrew. Calming her thoughts, she strode down the hallway and entered the kitchen.

"That didn't take long," Andrew said.

"He's almost asleep already. He had a fun day today. Thanks for giving him so much attention."

"You don't have to thank me. I enjoy it."

She pictured JJ and Andrew at the beach, too cold to swim, but running along in the sand throwing a ball back and forth. The Indian-summer afternoon had been free and fun, but the morning had been different, and she fell silent as the image pelted through her mind.

Andrew frowned as he watched her.

"You're right," Hannah said, sitting across from him. "It's not just Philip and Jemma talking. People are gossiping. I saw the looks in church today. They look at me, then at you with arched eyebrows. I know what they're thinking, and I have to stop it."

"Don't worry about me, Hannah."

"But I do. It's wrong for me to hide behind you to avoid telling people the truth. I was raped. I have to face it."

"You have faced it. It's—"

"No, I haven't." Her stomach knotted with the truth. "I've avoided it. I didn't have the courage to tell you when I should have. I still haven't told Annie, and she's one of my best friends. She knows. I can see it in her face, but she hasn't said a word. How do you think this baby would feel knowing that I'm ashamed of it?"

Tears bubbled in her eyes, and she felt them roll down her cheeks. Irritated, she brushed them away with the back of her hand. "I'm hurting an unborn child with my attitude."

Andrew grasped a paper napkin from the holder and brushed her cheek. "Don't blame yourself for this. You're the innocent victim. When the baby's born, you'll lavish him with love."

"Him?"

He gave a half shrug. "Him. Her." His head lowered as if in thought. "You'll love the baby. I can't imagine anything else."

"But what about you, Andrew?"

"I can handle gossip. I have for—"

Her heart rose to her throat. "This isn't about the gossip. What about you and the baby?"

His look sent chills down her back. She sensed she'd asked a question that he'd been pondering, and she feared hearing the answer now that she'd asked.

Andrew took her hand in his, then raised it to his lips

and kissed her fingers. "You know I care about you more than words can say."

"I'd hoped."

He nodded, then lowered his eyes again. "I've struggled with the situation. I'm not going to lie."

The chill turned into frozen fear. Why had she asked? She couldn't bear to lose Andrew now, not when she'd let her heart go wild. She loved him. The three words rang in her head. *She loved him.*

"You look frightened, Hannah. Don't be."

What did he mean? Hadn't he realized their lives had woven into a strong, beautiful tapestry? If he pulled away, he would leave her in shreds.

Andrew's look softened. He lifted a finger and brushed it along her jaw, then caressed her cheek. His hand felt warm against her cold flesh. "Let me finish. I've struggled with the situation, but when Philip talked to me, I realized that I didn't care about the baby's father, I cared about you. If something good came out of my words with Philip, it was that. I'm here for the long haul, Hannah, and once the confusion settles down, we need to do some talking."

"Talking?"

"About us."

Her pulse escalated. "There's so much to consider, and I'm frightened."

"Frightened about us?"

"No. Jack. He'll be released in a couple of days."

"I know. I've had the same thought."

He rose and drew her into his arms. "We'll be on guard, Hannah. That's all we can do."

"But if he finds out about the baby, he'll—"

"Don't even think about it. We have a couple of days.

What do you say? We'll handle the problems as they arise."

She couldn't say anything because his lips met hers, and her fears slipped to the back of her mind. In their place, her defeated spirit lifted like a kite on the wind as he kissed her gently.

Hannah pulled her hand from the receiver, praying her arrangement to talk with Jemma had been the right one. If Philip and Andrew were at odds over her, then she had to resolve it. She'd thought about it since Sunday, wondering what to do. This seemed the only answer.

Jemma had agreed to meet her at the coffee shop down the street, and since Jemma needed a while to get there, Hannah used the extra time to unload the dishwasher. While she stacked plates and bowls in the cabinet, her thoughts drifted to her talk with Andrew and then to the calendar hanging beside the kitchen phone. October fifth. Jack would be released today.

Fear suddenly grabbed her. Would he come after her or JJ again? As much as she wanted to think he'd learned a lesson, she knew Jack would learn nothing. His goal was to force her back into his life, and she'd rather die than allow JJ to be influenced or abused by his father.

As the possibility tore through her mind, a plate slipped from her hand and shattered on the floor. Her fingers shaking, she picked up the larger pieces, then wet a paper towel to capture the smaller fragments. When she dropped them into the trash, a red splotch appeared on the white towel.

She studied her finger and saw a sliver of china imbedded in her middle finger while blood oozed around the wound. Jack, too, was like this—a shard in her life, making her bleed physically and emotionally. She had to stop him, but how?

As she headed for the bathroom medicine cabinet, a prayer wove through her mind. She needed constant prayer. She couldn't waver in her determination to ask for the Lord's help. He was the only One who could remove Jack from their lives. JJ and this baby deserved lives of safety and security. With Jack around, they had none.

Hannah rinsed her hand, dabbed on an antiseptic, then withdrew a plastic bandage strip and wrapped it around her finger. Moving away from Loving entered her thoughts as she pressed on the adhesive, but the idea pained her. Life had become complete since she'd met Andrew.

With Andrew still in her thoughts, Hannah glanced at her watch, realizing she should be on her way. She grabbed a comb and pulled it through her hair, then checked the bandage to make sure she'd stopped the bleeding.

With her bag draped over her shoulder, she headed down the stairs and outside into the temperate air. Autumn had arrived. The crisper air felt warm in the sunlight, but in the shade, a chilly breeze wrapped across her frame.

She hurried down the sidewalk, glancing at her reflection in the store windows. At the coffee shop, she grasped the doorknob, gave it a pull and stepped inside. The warmth felt good as she looked around until she spotted Jemma seated at a booth on the side wall.

Jemma gave her a wave, and she crossed over, trying to look normal when all she could think of was the purpose for this visit.

"Thanks for coming," Hannah said, sliding into the booth across from her. "I know it was quick notice."

"That's what's nice about having a retired husband. He's often home to babysit." Jemma gave her a sweet smile, but behind her eyes a questioning look grew. She lowered her gaze to Hannah's bandage. "You cut your finger."

"Just careless. Nothing serious." She tucked her hand in her lap, not wanting to talk about Jack and his release.

The waitress arrived and served them coffee, and Hannah took a moment to gather her wits before initiating the subject. "How are the children?" she asked.

A frown flickered across Jemma's face. "They're fine." She shifted her saucer closer to her. "Is JJ okay?"

"He's fine." Hannah realized she needed to get to the topic. "This isn't about JJ."

Jemma's head tilted downward, but her eyes kept their direct gaze. "So what is this about? You wanted my opinion."

"It's more than an opinion, Jemma. I want to explain something." Hannah swallowed her discomfort and took a lengthy breath. "You know that I'm pregnant." Her hand, unbidden, caressed her belly.

Jemma's head jerked upward as a look of surprise filled her face. "I figured you were."

"And so do many of the women in the congregation. I see them looking at me and Andrew."

"Yes."

She didn't deny it, and Hannah was relieved she was being honest. "Andrew's not the baby's father, Jemma."

Her intake of air resounded in Hannah's ears.

"What do you mean?" Jemma asked. "If he's not, then who—"

"The baby is Jack's."

"But I thought you were divor—"

"He used to rape me, and the night I ran from the house he forced me to be with him again."

"Raped you?" Jemma's mouth wrenched downward as her eyes searched Hannah's.

"He's a strong man, and he'd been drinking. When he's mean, I can't stop him. He beat me and then had his way. When he'd finished, he rolled over and fell asleep. I lay there, fearing to move, until he began to snore. Then I crept from the bed, grabbed a coat and JJ from his bed, and left the house, vowing it would never happen again. He'd taken my car keys, and I didn't want to make noise trying to find them so we walked. You know the rest of the story."

Jemma nodded, her shock fading to concern. "Hannah, I'm so sorry. You've been through so much, and then we all thought that—"

"That Andrew was the father. Believe me. Andrew has given me friendship and support. He's done nothing improper. He'd never even suggested it."

"I'm so sorry. It's not my business, but Philip likes you and thought that Andrew wasn't being responsible. That he'd—"

"Philip owes Andrew an apology. Andrew was protecting me by not telling him what had happened. I don't want to make this a public announcement, so I guess those who are speculating will continue to blame Andrew."

Jemma shook her head. "It's a bad situation for you and Andrew, but I'll respect your wishes, Hannah. I won't tell anyone…except Philip. I hope you don't mind."

"I want Philip to know. Andrew isn't aware that I'm telling you this. I suppose he'll be angry."

"He'll understand. I'm disappointed that Philip

jumped to conclusions. I warned him that he should learn the truth before saying anything, but you know men. And the Somerville name. Philip does have a problem with pride."

"We all do, I suppose. If I weren't so proud, I'd spread the word about what happened."

"Maybe little by little you will, Hannah. I hope you've told some of your friends. I pray the police knew this."

Hannah shook her head, wishing she'd been honest with them, but now it was too late. Jack was free again which meant she wasn't.

"Here's my school," JJ called from the back seat.

Andrew chuckled at the boy's excitement about returning to his school late in the day for the fall open house and festival. He turned into the parking lot. "You like kindergarten, JJ?"

JJ gave two strong nods. "We have fun homework."

"Fun homework? I hope you always feel that way, pal," Andrew said, seeing Hannah's warm smile.

He pulled into a parking slot and turned off the ignition. JJ unhooked his seat belt and unlatched the door before Andrew had a chance to get out. He grinned, witnessing the boy's new sense of grown-up independence.

Hannah stepped outside, her protruding belly clearly evident beneath her oversized top. She caught JJ's arm. "I want you to stay close to us, JJ. It's dusky. Do you hear me?"

"But today's my birthday. I'm five and I wanna see the scarecrows and pick out a pumpkin. And I get a treat, too."

"We'll do that together," Hannah said, taking his hand as they walked through the parking lot.

Andrew understood Hannah's unspoken fear. Jack had been released, and they'd both talked around the subject without dealing with it.

What they had dealt with was Hannah's visit to Jemma ten days earlier. At first, Andrew had been angry. Then he'd realized Hannah's unselfish desire to smooth things over between him and Philip. He couldn't fault her for that. Philip had apologized and their relationship had healed once again.

"Here's the scarecrow contest," Andrew said, steering them toward the display created by the elementary school classes.

"I see mine," JJ said, running toward the entrance.

"Hold up," Andrew called, his gaze darting around the periphery, watching for Jack's surprise attack, but the way seemed clear.

At the entrance to the roped-off section, Andrew picked up a flyer and scanned it. "Pumpkin decorating and scarecrows."

"And you vote for the best one," JJ said, bouncing in place as if he couldn't wait one more minute.

Andrew lifted his head from the flyer. "The winning class will be taken on a field trip to the corn maze. They'll learn about varieties of corn, gourds and pumpkins the flyer says."

Hannah shook her head. "What's a corn maze?"

"Mom," JJ said as if he couldn't believe she wouldn't know.

His look made them both chuckle.

"My teacher Mrs. Daily said it's a path through the corn, and we find prizes."

"Then let's hope you win," Andrew said, as he waved them into the contest area. He leaned closer to Hannah. "The flyer tells all about the corn maze. I'll show you later."

She grinned and followed him into the exhibit.

As they made their way through the aisle, Andrew searched the crowd. He couldn't dislodge the uneasiness he felt. He could only imagine Hannah's constant worry, trying to live each day with the continual threat.

Andrew tried to forget his fears as they viewed the children's ingenious creations—pumpkin and burlap heads wearing old coveralls and flannel shirts.

When JJ dashed to his class's scarecrow, Andrew and Hannah followed.

"It's great," Andrew said, eyeing the paper sack head with the crude misplaced drawings of eyes, nose, mouth and ears.

"Let's vote for this one," Hannah said. "I like it best."

JJ beamed. "Me, too."

They cast their votes, then made their way to the pumpkin patch and to the tables where they used colorful markers to create a hand-designed pumpkin face. Andrew stuck the decorated pumpkin in the crook of his arm, then captured JJ's hand in his as the boy tugged him toward the captivating scent of cider and donuts.

"Aren't you tired, boy?" Andrew asked, anxious to get moving and find a place to talk with Hannah alone. "We're having cake and ice cream after dinner."

"I'm not tired," he said. "It's my birthday, remember?"

Hannah gave her son a weary look. "Okay, but this is our last stop. You're starting to slow down."

In truth, Hannah had slowed down. Andrew located an empty bale of hay where Hannah sat while they went to purchase the treats. Before JJ finished his large do-nut, he'd slid down and used what remained of Hannah's lap for a pillow.

"Just as I thought, JJ. Sit up."

"But, Mommy. I'm comfortable."

Then to Andrew's surprise, JJ suddenly lurched up-ward and gaped at Hannah. "What was that?"

She laughed. "The baby moved."

JJ leaned down to stare at her belly. "It moved? How come?"

"The baby just moves sometimes."

"Maybe I squashed him?"

Andrew drew closer, intrigued by the event. "You're feeling him move?"

"Of course."

"Feel it, Andrew," JJ said, grasping his hand and pulling him toward Hannah's abdomen.

He eyed Hannah, then JJ, and hesitated.

"Go ahead," JJ said, urging his hand forward.

Hannah nodded, and Andrew accepted the offer and rested his palm against her rounded stomach. Nothing happened.

JJ watched his hand. "Do you feel him? He kicked me."

"I guess he went back to sleep," Andrew said, amazed at his disappointment. He started to pull his hand away, but Hannah captured it and held it in place.

"Don't move," she said.

With pure amazement, Andrew felt a rolling sensa-tion beneath his hand, then suddenly a vigorous poke that whacked against his palm.

"A foot or an elbow," Hannah said, her voice send-ing ripples down Andrew's spine.

"That's truly awesome."

"It makes you realize there's a little human being living in there where it's safe."

Where it's safe. Andrew raised his head, and his focus shifted to the crowd. He scanned the area and saw nothing suspicious.

His hand still tingled as they headed back to the car with JJ dragging along behind them.

As he guessed would happen, JJ drifted to sleep as soon as the sedan rolled out onto the highway. He basked in the quiet for a minute, reliving the wonderful experience of feeling the baby move beneath his hand.

Hannah leaned her head against the seat back, and Andrew feared she'd drift off, too, before he had time to talk with her. He sent up a prayer that God's will be done.

"Do you feel like talking?" he asked. His hands clasped the steering wheel tighter than he had realized, and he forced himself to loosen his grip.

"Sure," she said, rolling her head toward him without lifting it.

"I've been thinking about us."

His comment brought her up straight, and she looked at him with a question in her eyes. Before he continued, he glanced into the back seat to make sure JJ slept soundly.

"About marriage."

"Marriage?"

He glanced at her, concerned about the tone of her voice. "Does that surprise you?"

"Yes, I guess it does."

"You don't seem happy, Hannah."

The look on his face saddened her. "I am, Andrew, but the timing's not good."

"Timing? What do you mean? It's perfect. We could get settled before the baby's born. We could buy a new house if you'd like and get a room ready for—"

"Andrew, things are so up in the air. Jack's been released, I'm expecting his child, people are gossiping. It just seems to me—"

"I'm not talking about Jack or gossiping, Hannah. I'm talking about marrying you and making a home together."

When she looked at him, tears filled her eyes. "Thank you. Thank you from the bottom of my heart, but I can't think of marriage until I feel more in control of my life again. I'm not ready, Andrew."

Andrew clenched his jaw to fight the dejection. He tried to comprehend Hannah's thinking, but he wasn't always successful. She set her mind, and nothing could sway her. His confidence slipped into a pit. She wasn't ready now, and he would try to understand that. But would she ever be ready? That was the question that left Andrew in despair.

"You said *no?*" Jenni's eyebrows arched, and she dropped the chocolate-covered spoon onto the work area. "Why would you refuse Andrew's proposal? He obviously cares about you."

"I know he cares, and I care about him." Care? She loved him, but… "But it's not the right time, Jenni. Think about it. Jack's out of jail. He could be at my door—"

"Right. And wouldn't it be wonderful to have Andrew by your side through all these problems?"

The vision of Andrew by her side settled over her like a cozy comforter, but she didn't want his pity. She feared Andrew's proposal had little to do with love and all to do with compassion. "Yes, but—"

"But? I don't get it, Hannah. He's every woman's dream. You'll never find a man more kind. And he's a true Christian."

"I need time for myself. Time to think through all that's happening. If Andrew marries me now, we'd only validate everyone's assumptions. They'd see the marriage as an admission of our guilt. I'm not up to dealing with that now. I want to get married because I'm ready—and Andrew's ready—and I know it's right." She flung her hands in the air, slinging melted chocolate from her spoon. She set the chocolate-covered utensil onto a spoon rack and grabbed a roll of paper towels.

"It's really because you don't trust, Hannah. You're just protecting yourself. Love is patient. It does not envy or boast. It isn't proud. It always protects, trusts, hopes, perseveres. How can you let your inability to trust stand in the way of love?"

"First Corinthians, I remember, it also says love rejoices in the truth, and there's a truth that's missing, Jenni."

Jenni's nose wrinkled with her frown. "Missing? I don't understand."

Hannah's heart rose to her throat. "Love isn't one-sided. Andrew's never said he loves me."

Hannah had watched Jenni's eyebrows shoot up earlier, but this time they reached her hairline.

"Never once?"

"Never once," she said, realizing how difficult it was to admit it aloud.

Jenni shifted closer and rested her hand on Hannah's shoulder. "But he does love you. It's obvious."

"How do I know it's not pity or Christian kindness? Andrew's been through a lot. He understands problems, and he's sympathetic to them. I don't want someone to marry me because it's a nice, pat way to solve a problem."

Jenni rolled her eyes. "Christians don't propose and marry out of kindness. They believe in the vows that they say at the wedding. To love and honor, remember?"

"He loves JJ. I'm confident of that," Hannah said. She remembered Andrew's awed reaction at JJ's school event. "He felt the baby move the other day. It was amazing to see."

"You mean JJ?"

"Both of them, but I meant Andrew. His face almost glowed."

"See. If that isn't love, I don't know what is."

Hannah didn't answer but turned off the burner, then lifted her pan of chocolate and carried it to the molds she'd laid out.

"Have you told anyone else besides Andrew's family and me?"

"About the proposal?"

"No, about what happened to you—that it's Jack's baby."

Hannah used the spoon to pour chocolate into the molds. "Yes, I told Annie. She wept."

"And I suppose she was disappointed that you hadn't told the police."

Hannah nodded. "But she understood, I think." She tried to concentrate on filling the chocolate molds, but her mind swam with thoughts. "My life is in turmoil, Jenni. I want to get married, but I want it to be joyful, not a relationship filled with fear of what will happen next. I need to give Jack time so I can tell if he's given up on us or if his torment will continue."

"That's a sad reason to refuse Andrew's proposal."

"Maybe you think it's sad, but I think it's the best thing to do." Hannah slid two molds onto a tray and smacked it against the worktable to settle the chocolate and remove the air bubbles.

With the thud, Jenni's arms dropped to her side with a look of frustration, but the telephone's peal halted the conversation. Jenni grabbed the phone, then stretched her arm toward Hannah. "It's for you. The school."

"The school?" Hannah's stomach tightened into a knot. *JJ.* She grasped the receiver. "Hello, this is Hannah Currey. Is something wrong?"

The woman's anxious voice set her on edge as she talked about recess. *Get to the point,* Hannah cried out in her mind. *Jack.* That's all she could think.

"He what?" She turned to Jenni, almost relieved at the woman's message. "JJ broke his arm on the playground at recess."

Chapter Fourteen

"What happened, pal?" Andrew asked when he came through the door.

JJ sat at the kitchen table, his arm in a cast.

"I'm grateful it was his left arm," Hannah said. Looking at Andrew's concerned face took her mind back to Jenni's comment. *Wouldn't it be wonderful to have Andrew by your side through all these problems?* At this moment, she knew Jenni had been right. The love Andrew had for JJ brimmed in his eyes.

"You can put your name on my cast with a marker," JJ said. "See? The doctor did." He pointed to the scrawl written across the plaster cast.

Andrew peered at the doctor's signature and pulled a chair beside JJ's. "I'll do that after you eat. So tell me what happened."

JJ told his story of how he'd climbed the ladder up the slide, but some roughhousing classmate had climbed up behind and pushed him off.

"Why would he do that?" Andrew asked, his face in a deep frown.

JJ's innocent gaze riveted to Andrew's. "He's mean to everyone. He pushes the girls even. Mom said no one should push a girl."

"Your mom's right, JJ. Everyone deserves to be treated with kindness and understanding. That's how God tells us to behave."

"Oh," JJ said, dragging out the word. He turned to Hannah. "But Daddy was mean to you, Mom."

Hannah's heart squeezed at the child's revelation, and she thanked God he saw the difference between what was right and what was wrong. "Dad made a bad mistake."

"He scares me," JJ said. "He says Jesus and God's name when he's mad. We shouldn't do that."

"That's right, sweetheart," Hannah said, touched by her son's awareness since he'd attended Sunday school.

"Do you say God's name when you're angry?" His gaze settled on Andrew.

"Never, JJ. I've done bad things in my life, but I never swear using God's name, and you won't, either."

"I won't either," JJ said. "I want to be like you when I grow up, Andrew. You're the best."

Andrew leaned down and kissed JJ's cheek. "So are you, pal. You and your mom are the very best."

He looked upward into Hannah's eyes, and it nearly broke her heart.

When Philip came through the Bay Breeze lobby, Andrew grasped the chance to talk with him. Since Hannah had refused his proposal, he'd been confused—disappointed or both. Today seemed a likely time to discuss his plan.

"Do you have a minute?" Andrew asked, striding

across the elegant carpet that covered the reception area's plank flooring.

"I have an hour," Philip said, grinning at him. He motioned to the center of the lobby where love seats and overstuffed chairs formed a conversation area.

"How about my office? It's more private there."

Philip agreed and followed him through the lobby and down the hallways into the office area. As they walked, he chatted about Ellie and Philip Junior, then invited Andrew and Hannah for dinner one evening.

"I'll check with Hannah," Andrew said, opening his office door and motioning Philip inside.

Instead of sitting behind his desk, Andrew joined Philip in one of the two chairs. "I've been giving some thought to the trust fund," he said.

Philip grinned. "Am I going to hear a wedding announcement?"

Andrew felt his spirit collapse, then related to Philip what had happened.

"You're kidding?"

"No, I'm dead serious. I'm disappointed and confused."

"And sad, I hope."

Andrew nodded, understanding the point Philip had made. "Yes, not just sad. Hurt, if I'm honest. I'd expected her to say yes."

"Women need to be wooed, you know. Flowers, candy, romance."

Andrew wavered. He'd never given Hannah flowers, and she made candy all day long. Andrew peered at his brother.

"I hope you've at least said I love you."

Andrew faltered. *I love you?* He'd couldn't recall saying the words, but he assumed Hannah knew that.

"From the look on your face, I'd guess you hadn't bothered."

"I don't remember. I thought she would understand how I felt."

Philip shook his head and leaned back in the chair. "You have a lot to learn, Andrew. Women never take love for granted. They want to hear it daily. She needs to know that you love her with all your heart."

"I do, and I tried to show her that even if I haven't said it, but maybe you're right."

"No maybe about it. Talk with Jemma if you don't believe me."

Andrew ran his hand across the back of his neck to relieve the stress. How stupid of him not to realize that love needed to be said as well as shown.

"So what about the trust fund? It's yours, you know that. You can do with it as you please, but I hope you're not leaving again since Hannah—"

"Leaving?" Andrew's comment disappointed him. "No. I won't do that again, Philip. You have my word. This is home, and I love Hannah, and I'm not giving up. I'll do whatever I can to convince her that I love her from the bottom of my feet to the top of my head."

Philip chuckled. "That should do it."

"Maybe not. Hannah says marriage right now isn't good timing." He told Philip all that had transpired. "The trust fund's not for me but for Hannah. She can use the money with the baby coming. She needs a house and a wholesome place for kids to play outside. I don't know if her insurance will cover—"

Philip waved his hand. "Have you talked this over with her?"

"No, but—"

"Second mistake. You've already told me how proud and independent she's always been. Ask her before doing anything rash. She's sensitive right now. Pregnancy brings out emotions women didn't even know they have. Ask her first. If she's in agreement, the money's yours. You don't have to ask me."

Ask Hannah. Andrew stared across his desk out the window and watched golden leaves fluttering to the ground. A sense of sadness washed over him. Hannah seemed as fragile as the dying leaf that fluttered past the window—a lone life flung on the breeze. Buoyed up, then dropped to the ground and trampled.

Had he ever told her he loved her? The question repeated itself in his head like a sad refrain.

Hannah pulled in front of the school, slipped the gear into Park and turned off the ignition. Her gaze focused on the entrance, watching for JJ. When she saw him bound outside, she unlocked the car door and slipped one foot to the ground as a hand clutched her window and another the door frame, blocking her inside the car.

"Glad to see me back, Hannah?" Jack leaned into her face, his liquored breath searing her lungs.

Her pulse raced. "Leave me alone, Jack. Haven't you learned anything?" She glanced toward JJ and saw him skitter back into the school. Thankfulness flooded her.

"You mean learned my lesson?" He grabbed her coat at the throat and dragged her closer. "Haven't you learned yours? You're my wife and JJ's my son. I'm coming back home to live with you."

Hannah prayed to stay calm. "You have no home with us. We're divorced. Or have you forgotten?" She yanked her coat over her belly to hide it from Jack's view.

"You have room for that new boyfriend though, huh? The rich guy."

"I have no boyfriend. He's a friend. JJ and I live alone." She wished she hadn't mentioned their son's name.

Jack's hand clamped on to her arm, and he dragged her upward. "JJ's my son, too. I have rights to see him."

"You have no rights." As he yanked her forward, she felt the air billow inside her coat, and Jack's eyes followed.

"No rights?" He veered backward without releasing his grip. "Well, looky here." He shifted his free hand and wrapped his palm around her belly. "Seems like your friend has his rights."

Her heart thudded with such speed Hannah could hardly breathe. She tried to jerk from his grasp, but he clamped down harder, and her arm ached with the pressure. "Let go, Jack. You're hurting me."

"I'll do more than hurt you, you tramp." He pulled his hand from her belly and tightened his grip on her jacket collar.

Anger burst inside her, and the words she'd tried to hide flew from her mouth. "This is your baby, Jack. Yours." She screamed into his face.

His gaze lowered again while a crooked grin appeared incongruent with his evil eyes. "Well, now, that's different." He gloated at her and eyed her abdomen. "I'm quite the man, don't you think?"

"I think you're an animal."

His maniacal laugh sent chills down her back.

"But a fertile one."

Her hope sank with each moment. "Please, Jack, leave me alone. Let me live my life, and you live yours. What do you want from me?"

"Whatever I can get."

He wanted her money and his own way with her. She struggled and turned her head away from his steely gaze. Why had she bothered to speak to him? *Lord help me. Tell me what to do.*

Jack let go of her collar and pulled her against him, his nose against hers, his lips moving against her mouth. "If you don't want me, I'll take JJ. How's that?"

Her legs trembled until she felt they wouldn't hold her up any longer. She had no words to say. Nothing would change Jack's mind. *God give me words.*

A police siren sounded in the distance, and as if the Lord had answered her prayers, words came. "I told JJ if he saw you he should tell someone to call the police, Jack. You'd better get out of here."

Rage spread across his face, and he pulled back his fist, but halted when the siren sounded closer. "Don't think you're finished with me, Hannah. You know JJ's mine. Do you hear me?" He let go and pivoted toward his car.

Hannah clung to the door frame and struggled to breathe.

He yanked open his car door. "And you're mine, too, Hannah. You and that kid in your belly."

He climbed into his car and tore off, leaving a black tread on the concrete.

The siren faded again, and Hannah thanked God for giving her the words that had caused Jack to run.

But nothing would stop him. She would call the police, but Jack would keep moving. He would change cars. He would evade the law. She'd seen the determination in his face. She needed to tell JJ if he saw his father to have someone call the police. She'd never told him. JJ would never be safe. She'd never be safe. Nothing would stop Jack. Nothing.

"What's wrong with JJ?" Andrew asked, stepping into Hannah's kitchen and hearing the boy's cry from another room.

"He's still upset about Jack, but now we have a new problem. They announced the winner of the scarecrow contest. A fourth-grade class won, and he's disappointed. He keeps bugging me to take him to the corn maze." She turned away and headed toward the door to the living room.

"That's not fair, really." Andrew dug his hands into his jacket pocket. "The five-year-olds can't compete against the older kids."

"No, but he'll have a chance to win another time. He has to learn to take defeat." Hannah had been living with defeat forever. She paused in the hall doorway. "Coming?"

Andrew nodded, but stood a moment after she left, thinking about JJ. By the time he entered the living room, JJ's crying had halted.

Hannah grinned. "He probably fell asleep."

Another issue dropped into Andrew's mind. "Have the police called you back?"

She shook her head. "They won't find Jack. He'll do anything to ditch them. He knows they're out for him this time."

"Don't be pessimistic, Hannah." Seeing her hopeless look tore at his heart, and though he had the same thoughts, he wanted to give her hope. "The police know how to deal with men like Jack. They'll find him and put him away again."

"Even if they do, he'll be back. I can't bear this anymore."

"Hannah." Andrew faltered, realizing this wasn't a good time to bring up the subject.

Her eyes searched his. "What?"

"What about drugs? Do you think Jack's problem is drugs?"

She lowered her eyes as her head drooped. "I never thought so, but what do I know?"

"That would explain how he's changed. Maybe your judgment wasn't bad after all."

"It was. I let myself believe. I hoped."

Tears brimmed her eyes, and Andrew drew her into his arms and held her close, feeling the baby press against his body. He longed to erase her bad memories as he'd longed to delete his own. And he had done that in a way. Since Hannah and JJ had filled his thoughts, his past problems had seemed less and less important.

The church gossip hadn't subsided, especially since Hannah's belly had grown too large to hide, but no one asked and no one said anything. He could live with that. He prayed Hannah could, too.

"Please don't cry, Hannah." He eased her away and curled his arm around her shoulders. "Let's sit for a minute. I've been thinking about something that will help."

She gave him a puzzled look, then settled beside him on the sofa. "I didn't mean to cry. I'm sorry. I hate self-pity and—"

"It's frustration, Hannah, not self-pity. You're determined and capable, but sometimes it's difficult to handle things we can't control."

"Like Jack."

He squeezed her hand. "Like Jack. We have to give that problem to the Lord."

Her head lifted, and her face brightened. "Did I tell you what happened when Jack had me cornered?"

"You did. The police sirens. You know the Lord works His way for us. Sometimes help isn't so obvious. We have to listen and hear His direction."

"Sometimes it's difficult." She squeezed his hand back.

He longed to kiss her, but the stressful moment extinguished his urge. "Speaking of listening to God's direction, I've been doing that."

"What do you mean?" She tilted her head.

"I may not have told you about my trust fund," he said.

Her puzzled look became a frown. "Trust fund? No, you haven't."

Andrew explained the fund and why he'd rejected it, then paused, concerned how she would react when he made his next suggestion.

"But your father forgave you or else he wouldn't have left you the money. Why would you refuse the gift?"

"I didn't earn it, and I didn't deserve it."

She shifted to face him squarely. "We haven't earned God's forgiveness either, and we don't deserve it, but every day you remind me that it's a gift out of the Father's love for His children, and we should accept it freely. Isn't this the same?"

Andrew's head jerked backward, startled by her analogy. He'd never compared his earthly father's forgiveness with the heavenly Father's. "It seems different."

"But it's not. Your father loved you despite what you did. So does the Lord. You've reminded me of that over and over. By refusing your father's trust fund, you're rejecting his forgiveness. If we don't accept God's gift, we're refusing salvation."

Hannah's words blew him away. He gazed at her, amazed at how she'd grown in faith since she'd begun attending worship and reading the Bible. Today her comparison impacted him.

"I've never looked at it that way, Hannah. Thank you for reminding me."

She sent him a full smile, the first he'd seen in days. "So what about this trust fund?" she asked.

"I want to give it to you."

Her smile vanished. "Give it to me? You're kidding."

"I'm not. You can use it for the baby. I want to marry you, Hannah, but if you won't accept my proposal, then I want to give you the next best thing."

"And that is…"

"The trust fund. Money so you can buy a house and pay the hospital bills."

She lowered her head and grew silent.

Her attitude puzzled him. He knew so little about women. "What's wrong?"

She inched her head upward, and her look disturbed him. "The next best thing isn't money, Andrew."

Confusion rolled over him. "Then what is it?"

She rose and shook her head. "One day you'll understand. I can't explain it to you."

"But—"

"Andrew!" JJ's voice pierced the tension, and he darted into the room and threw himself on Andrew. "We lost the contest."

"I heard. Sorry, pal, but maybe you'll win next year." He tousled the boy's hair, hoping to make him smile.

"But I wanted to go to the corn maze." His eyes

shifted toward Hannah. "Mom said I can't." He flung himself from Andrew's arms to the sofa.

Andrew had never seen the boy behave this way. "You won't get anything by pouting, JJ."

His lip shrunk back a tad. "But—"

Andrew rested his hand on the child's shoulder. "When you want something, you have to ask nicely and compromise."

"What's that?"

"Compromise? That means you give something to get something."

The child's face wrinkled. "But what can I give?"

"I don't know. Something you should do for your mom as a thank you."

JJ glanced at Hannah, then back to Andrew. "What?"

"Like picking up your toys," Hannah said, "or saying thank you instead of whining, eating vegetables when they're on your plate, keeping your room neat."

"I can put my toys away." JJ leaped from the sofa and grabbed an armload of toys, then vanished down the hall. Before Andrew could comment, the boy dashed back into the room and gathered up the rest of the mess.

Hannah stared at the hallway while Andrew listened to the sounds emanating from JJ's room.

"I know he just turned five," she said, "and he's gotten rambunctious since he started school."

"You probably told him when he was five he'd be a big boy. He'll calm down once he adjusts. He's excited." He stood and crossed the floor to stand beside her. "What do you say? Tomorrow's Saturday. Can we take him in the afternoon? He's trying to behave. Listen to him in there."

"You're spoiling him." Though she tried to sound firm, he heard the happiness in her voice.

"Never hurts to be spoiled. I'm trying to spoil you but you won't let me."

"I'm realistic," she said, resting her hand on his shoulder and gazing into his eyes. "Thank you," she said, standing on tiptoe so her lips could reach his.

He drew her closer and relished the scent of her fragrance. His fingers sought her wispy curls, and the silky threads caressed his palm while his mouth caressed her lips.

When he released her, he gave a nod toward JJ's room. "If the room looks good, what do you say?"

A wry grin crept over her. "Okay. This time."

Saturday afternoon, JJ bounded down the stairs and skipped along the sidewalk to Andrew's sedan. Despite JJ's cheer, no matter where they went, Andrew found himself scanning the area like a searchlight.

With everyone safely in the car, he followed the directions in the flyer he'd picked up at the school autumn fair and headed toward the farming community. JJ chattered from the back seat, leaving Andrew no time to convince Hannah to take the trust fund. She hadn't given him a yes or no, but her look said no.

Outside of town, the highway narrowed and, on each side of the road, fields spread to the horizon, now-barren ruts waiting for spring planting. In the distance, acres of yellowed corn stalks towered above the car, and soon a sign came into view off the shoulder advertising Shawn Farms Corn Maze. JJ's excitement mounted as the farm grew closer.

Andrew maneuvered his way through the busy parking lot as people returned to their cars or headed for the admission booth. Pumpkins grew on vines along the path; and near the entrance, a large area was heaped with pumpkins for sale. Indian corn and gourds hung in an exhibit with name placards like: speckled swan, cala- bash, black amber, and fiesta. Children gathered around them inspecting the display.

At the booth, Andrew paid the admission, and the clerk handed him a map. "Follow the maze—we have seventeen acres here—and at these points," she indi- cated a mark on the paper, "you'll find the answer to these questions. If you answer all the questions, you'll receive a free pumpkin and a discount coupon for dinner."

"Dinner," JJ said, rubbing his tummy.

Hannah gave him a playful poke, and Andrew pointed the way to the entrance.

"Did she say seventeen acres?" Hannah asked lag- ging behind him.

He'd forgotten the extra weight she carried. "Yes, but look." He showed her on the map. "There's an escape route."

Hannah looked at the paper and chuckled. "It's called Chicken Alley."

"Cluck, cluck," JJ said, flapping his arms.

Enjoying the warmth of the Indian-summer day, An- drew guided them into the maze, making wrong turns and running into dead ends, though they followed the guide sheet.

"Here's a clue," Hannah said, pointing to the placard that answered one of the questions. They studied the question list and penciled in the answer.

"This way," Andrew said, but when he turned around JJ had vanished.

"JJ!" Hannah shouted at the same time he'd noticed.

She spun around, peering into the heavy rows of towering corn stalks. "JJ!"

Andrew felt his pulse kick up a notch, and he darted to the next corner and looked around the heavy barrier of stalks. Another family headed his way, but when he asked, they hadn't seen a lone child.

Andrew controlled his panic and cupped his hands around his mouth. "JJ, either you come out now or we're heading home."

A rustling sound came from the stalks, and JJ appeared with a disappointed look on his face. "I was hiding. You were supposed to find me."

"Don't ever do that again, young man," Hannah said, grasping his arm. "It's not funny."

JJ's plaintive look aimed at Andrew.

"Your mother's not fooling, pal. No hiding. If you get lost in here, we'd never find you."

The boy hung his head and kicked at the fallen cobs lying on the ground.

"Let's go." Andrew beckoned him, and he followed along, soon forgetting they'd reprimanded him.

After nearly an hour had passed and they'd answered only nine of the twenty questions, Andrew eyed Chicken Alley on the map and suggested they make their escape. Hearing JJ's disappointed protests, he relented and they kept going.

A few minutes passed with more wrong turns until finally Andrew saw another answer. "Here's the next one," he said. Hannah pulled out the pencil, eyed the placard, and jotted down the answer, but when they turned back, JJ hadn't followed.

"Not again," Hannah said, frustration ringing in her voice. "JJ, this is it. We're leaving."

Nothing.

Andrew knelt and peered through the stalks where the branches were sparser, but he saw no sign of JJ. "Let's go back," he said, hurrying down the row and around the corner.

The aisle was empty.

He spun around and headed in the other direction. "JJ!"

"JJ!" Hannah's call reverberated through the stalks from the next row. "Do you see him?" she cried.

"No," he said, then spotted a couple turning the corner ahead of him. "Have you seen a five-year-old boy in that direction?"

The couple shook their heads. "It's easy to lose them in here," the father said, shooing his two little ones ahead of them.

"You'll find him," the woman said as they passed.

"JJ!" Andrew bellowed.

No response again.

Hannah rushed to him, her face filled with panic. "This isn't like him. He knew I meant business."

"He's here," Andrew said, calming her, yet realizing his own fear. They darted up the next aisle, keeping track of which way they had turned. An opening to Chicken Alley was ahead, and Andrew prayed he'd find JJ there.

"JJ!" they yelled in unison. "JJ!"

Andrew halted to listen, but all he heard was his pulse throbbing in his temple.

"JJ!" Hannah screamed.

A bird fluttered from the corn stalks.

"JJ!"

Andrew listened again and heard nothing.

Chapter Fifteen

Hannah grasped Andrew's arms, overcome with terror. She lowered her face into her hands, tears surging into her eyes. "I can't take this anymore, Andrew."

Andrew drew her into his arms. "We'll find him, Hannah. I know you're frightened, but it has to be something simple. He got distracted and wandered off."

She wanted to believe him, but something inside her sent a warning signal. A mother's instinct, maybe, but he couldn't convince her not to worry.

"We'll check Chicken Alley. According to the map, it's right here on the other side of this row," Andrew said, "and then we'll head back the way we came. He's probably waiting for us."

She gazed at the stalks soaring above her head and wondered how JJ felt wandering around in them lost. Seventeen acres would be overwhelming for a five-year-old.

Andrew nudged her toward the escape route as another family appeared from the opposite direction.

"We've lost my son," Hannah said. "He's five. Did you see him?"

The woman shrugged. "We didn't see a lost child." She grinned at the man beside her. "But a short time ago, we watched a man carrying a boy about that age along Chicken Alley. We were just talking about it."

"A man?" Panic heightened as Hannah feared her worst dream had come true.

"We laughed," the man said. "The kid was kicking and squirming like he didn't want to leave."

Hannah gasped.

"We figured the parents had had enough corn stalks for one day," the man said. "We're beginning to feel the same way."

"Do you have a photograph of JJ, Hannah?" Andrew asked, motioning to her shoulder bag.

Her hands trembled as she pulled out her wallet and the picture she carried inside it. She handed the snapshot to the couple.

"It's hard to tell," the woman said.

"He has a broken left arm," Hannah said. "You would notice that."

The man shook his head. "We saw him from the back, but he did have dark hair, kind of curly like yours."

The woman touched her husband's arm. "The man was medium height and stocky. He wore a plaid shirt, if that helps."

Hannah's heart fell. "Jack. It was Jack."

Andrew wrapped his arm around her waist. "Don't jump to conclusions, Hannah, please."

"It might not be your son," the woman said, handing her back the photo. "We're really sorry."

"Thanks," Andrew said.

Hannah nodded, unable to speak. Her voice had lodged in her throat and saying the name would only release her pent-up horror. Jack. His voice rang through her head. *JJ's my son, too. I have rights to see him.* But worse, she remembered asking him what he wanted from her. His answer charged through her mind. *Whatever I can get.* Did he really want JJ that badly?

"Let's go to the admissions booth," Andrew said, taking her hand. "Maybe someone found him...or they'll help us look."

He drew her forward into Chicken Alley, and she hurried the best she could to keep step beside him.

When they neared the booth, JJ wasn't there, and nausea crawled up Hannah's throat. The clerk seemed busy handing out a prize to one of the customers, but Andrew didn't wait his turn.

"We're looking for a lost five-year-old," Andrew said, leaning around the other man at the booth. "A boy."

Hannah delved into her pocket and pulled out the photograph. "He looks like this."

The customer tilted the photo in his direction. "I saw that kid a few minutes ago with a man. They were heading out, but the boy obviously didn't want to go."

"Jack's kidnapped him," Hannah said, her voice out of control.

"Kidnapped?" The clerk's voice raised as her eyes glazed with disbelief. "We've never had a problem here, and we've been running this event for eight years."

"It's the boy's father," Andrew said, "but we need to call the police. There's a protection order against him."

"Maybe I was wrong," the customer said. "Does your boy have a broken arm?"

Tears welled in Hannah's eyes, hearing the confirmation. "Yes. His left arm."

The man only nodded and stepped back.

The woman in the booth gasped and shoved the cell phone toward Andrew. "Do you want to call?"

"No. Please. I have a phone, but just make the call."

Their conversation sounded distant to Hannah. The sound muffled with the hum in her ears and the thump of her heart. Her legs weakened, and she clung to Andrew's arm.

"We'll sit over there until the police come," Andrew said. He supported her to a straw bale where she eased herself down.

Andrew sat beside her. "He wouldn't hurt JJ, Hannah. He's the boy's father."

She covered her face in her hands, feeling faint, and gasped for air. "He'll do anything to get back at me. He wants money. Maybe he thinks he can get money from me to get JJ back, but he should know I don't have any."

"But I do, Hannah. Do you think he knows that?"

Jack's words shot through her memory. *You have room for that new boyfriend though, huh? The rich guy.* "He knows about you. He called you a rich guy, but I don't know if he would ask for ransom."

Andrew wrapped his arm around her. "Money means nothing to me. I'll do anything for JJ's safety. Anything."

Hannah's hands trembled uncontrollably as she tried to insert the key in the outside lock. "Here," she said to Andrew, handing it to him.

He took the key from her and opened the door, then followed her up the stairs. At the top, he opened the apartment door.

She'd avoided stopping to tell Claire in the shop. Why make her panic? She'd tell her later. Hannah's prayers rose that the police would catch Jack today. He didn't have time to change cars, and he'd gotten away only a few minutes before they noticed JJ missing.

Then she remembered how much time they'd wasted searching for JJ in the cornstalks and waiting for the police. Jack could head toward U.S. 31 and be in Indiana or Illinois in less than two hours.

"I'm petrified," Hannah said. "I can't imagine what he'll do. I want to think he won't hurt JJ, but I don't trust Jack anymore. He'll do anything to get back at me."

"I told you, Hannah, I'll do anything in my power to get JJ back. I love the kid."

She looked into his fear-filled eyes. "I know you do."

She dropped her handbag on the kitchen counter and drew in a lengthy breath. "I feel as if I could sleep for a week, but I know I won't sleep at all."

"I'm not leaving you alone tonight. Let's see if you can stay with Jenni or—"

"I'm not leaving here. Jack or the police may call."

"Then we'll get someone to stay with you. Maybe Claire. I'll go down just before closing and tell her what happened."

Hannah nodded. "I doubt if Jack'll show up here, but I pray he calls." She gestured toward the phone, and as she did, her gaze fell on the answering machine and the steady blink signaling a message. Her pulse charged as she motioned to the red flashing light.

Andrew moved closer and pressed the button. "You have one message. Message one: October twenty-second, 2:37 p.m."

Andrew drew Hannah into his arms.

"This is Jack, Hannah," his hoarse voice rasped through the line. "Are you happy to hear my voice?" He let out a cackle as JJ's cry punctured the line.

Hannah gasped.

Jack's voice became muffled, but Hannah could make out his telling JJ to shut up. "Okay, listen. If you wanna see the boy again…" His voice distorted as static crackled through the line.

"I can't hear you," Hannah screamed.

Andrew eased her head onto his shoulder, his breathing heavy and irregular.

"That's the deal, Hannah. It's in your pretty little soft hands. Me, you, JJ and that new baby can make a home together if you call off the cops. If not, JJ and I will fend for ourselves, and you'll never see him again." He chuckled again. "You think about it, Hannah. If you want to see our son, you'll…" His voice faded with the bad connection, then rose in a spurt of laughter.

Then Hannah heard a click, cutting off his disturbing cackle, and she clung to Andrew, not knowing what to do or which way to turn. "I don't know what he said. I couldn't hear him."

"You know what he wants, Hannah." Desperation filled his voice.

She shook her head. "I want my son back, but I can't live that way any—"

"We'll call the police. They'll come up with a plan."

Hannah sank into a nearby chair while Andrew called the police station and relayed what had happened. When he finished, he turned on the kettle and urged her into the living room.

"I'll fix you some tea. You need to rest," he said as he eased her onto the sofa.

She leaned her head against the cushion, tears rolling down her cheeks in wracking sobs. Nothing would keep her from finding JJ. Visions rose in her mind of JJ's fright and Jack's violence. She'd never thought that she could murder anyone, but today the thought had entered her mind.

"Forgive me, Lord," she whispered aloud. "Give me strength and courage to bear this horrible situation. Be with JJ. Dearest Lord, keep him safe. Thank you for Andrew. What would I do without him?"

"Sorry," Andrew said walking toward her, carrying two mugs. "I didn't hear what you said."

"I was praying."

He handed her a mug, then bent down to kiss the top of her head. "I've been praying all afternoon. The Lord will protect him, Hannah. He has to."

Andrew sat beside her and rested his hand on her belly. She felt the baby shift and saw the awed wonder on Andrew's face.

"That little one is stressed out, too." He slipped his arm around her shoulders and drew her closer. "Hannah, I've been thinking. I know you resent the trust-fund idea, but since you don't want it and neither do I, what do you think about offering a ransom for JJ. You said it yourself. Jack loves money. He'll take the money and give us back JJ."

Hannah's chest tightened, hearing Andrew's words. *Give us back JJ.* Andrew's love for her son had become so evident, so unselfish. She placed a palm on each side of his face and gazed into his eyes. "Thank you for being so generous, but you know money won't stop Jack. It would be gone in a flash, and he'd be back for more."

His gaze lowered, and Hannah could almost hear him thinking. When he looked at her, he rested his hands against her cheeks as his lips moved to hers. His kiss radiated sweet longing, and she felt tears well in her eyes. When dampness dripped to her fingers, she opened her eyes and saw Andrew's tearful sorrow.

"Hannah, I love you more than words can say. I love JJ. I pray that when he's back you'll reconsider my proposal. I don't want to live without you. You, JJ and even the little one who's been kicking at my hand mean everything to me. Please don't answer. Just remember what I'm saying."

I love you more than words can say. He loved her. The words rolled over her like a balm. She'd longed to hear him say it, and today in the midst of a nightmare her dream had been answered. She answered him with a lingering kiss, then stayed in his arms, waiting for the police to arrive.

"I didn't think anything could top Jack's abuse, Jenni," Hannah said, "but today has been the worst one of my life." Her thoughts slipped back to Andrew's words. "Still I like to think God always has a purpose for everything that happens. I don't blame the Lord for this. I know Satan roams the earth and sways people to do wrong, but something good has come of this horrible experience."

A puzzled look spread across Jenni's face. "Something good?" Her voice sounded skeptical.

Hannah nodded. "Today, Andrew told me he loves me."

Jenni's face brightened. "He did! I knew it." She rose from her crouched position beside Hannah. "I knew he'd tell you eventually, because it's so obvious he loves you. Sometimes men don't realize how much women love to hear those three little words."

"I thought my heart would burst when he said it, but the good feeling lasted only a second until JJ filled my mind again." Hannah ran her fingers over her temples to soothe the pressure. "Jenni, you're right. I have to think clearly. Where would Jack go to hide JJ?" She rose, propping up her belly with her left hand.

"Can you call someone? What about his family?"

"I never really knew Jack's family." But Jenni had set Hannah's mind in motion.

Jenni picked up her purse and slung it over her shoulder. "Claire should be up here in a minute." She eyed her watch. "It's closing time so I'll get going, but think about those things. Jack's friends or coworkers, maybe someone will have an idea."

Hannah nodded, facing how little she really knew about Jack. She'd rarely met his friends and had never had a real relationship with the few family members he had. "I'll be fine, Jenni. Thanks."

She walked Jenni to the door and watched her descend the stairs. When she stepped outside, Hannah turned and locked the door behind her.

Can you call someone? Jenni's words struck her. Hannah wandered to a kitchen chair, sorting out the possibilities. Someone had to know where Jack was. She pressed her fingers against her aching eyes, then moved them to her temples. She made small circles, trying to ease the thud of her pulse.

Someone knew. Someone. Jack's friends? She didn't know them. His family? She didn't know them either, except his brother. His brother. Maybe.

Hannah rose and opened the kitchen drawer. Inside, she located her personal address book. Was Jack's brother listed? She opened the ledger and turned to the *C*s. Sam Currey. Her pulse skipped when she saw the phone number.

She stepped to the wall phone, trembling as she pushed the number pads, and held her breath as it rang. Perspiration covered her palm, yet her hands felt cold. Third ring. Fourth ring. No answering machine. Sixth ring. Seventh ring. She pulled the phone from her ear and hung up.

Later. She'd try again later. She braced her belly and pressed her free hand against her aching back as she headed through the kitchen doorway.

In the living room, she stared out the front window, looking down on Washington. Traffic was light for a Saturday evening. Reflected in the street lights, a few leaves skittered across Washington Street on the breeze, but the downtown left little room for trees and grass.

She longed for a real home for JJ and now the baby— a home where they could have a yard and maybe a pet. Andrew had offered her that home with his proposal, and now that he'd said he loved her and she'd begun to believe him, Hannah desperately wanted to accept his offer of marriage. But not until JJ was home safely.

Hannah turned from the window and sank onto the sofa, resting her head on the cushion. Andrew had given her so much. Besides friendship, he'd offered support and, most important, had helped her renew her faith. He'd taught her that despite life's failings, God never gave up on His children.

When she'd learned about Andrew's past, the details had surprised her—in truth, upset her—since she wondered if he would slip back into that mold again. Jack had seemed like an all-right guy until his true character arose from beneath his disguise. She'd misjudged Jack. She'd been duped into a marriage that was doomed. Looking back, Hannah had seen the signs, but she hadn't wanted to believe them. She'd thought a life with Jack would be better than the life of poverty and loneliness she'd been leading. She'd been so wrong.

All Hannah had wanted was to be truly loved. How long did it take her to realize that God truly loved her? He had not given up on her or betrayed her. The Lord had been her shelter and shield, and she'd let Him down. And Andrew. He'd tried to stick by her side, support her, and love her, but she hadn't believed it. She'd let him down, too, by refusing his proposal.

Thank you, Father, for so many blessings, but today I need Your help again. I want to find my son. Make my life complete once more. You've given me a man to love me unselfishly and a new baby to raise knowing You are the Almighty and the giver of all good gifts. Now please give me back my son. Protect him until—

A sob erupted from Hannah's throat. God knew her needs. She'd asked. Now she had to have faith.

She rested her head against the sofa cushion, allowing the prayer to give her strength. Time ticked past, and finally she rose again, knowing that Claire would arrive soon.

She returned to the kitchen and opened her phone directory. This time with courage, she punched in Sam Currey's telephone number. One ring. Two. Three. Then, Sam's rough voice came across the wire,

Hannah caught her breath. "I'm looking for Jack," she said without identifying herself, trying to sound calm.

"You and everyone," Sam muttered.

Everyone? "This is Hannah, Sam. I—"

"I don't know nothin'." He dropped the receiver and disconnected.

A lump rose to Hannah's throat, and she bit her lip

trying to decide what to do. She'd prayed that the Lord give her strength, so why would she falter now with God on her side? She drew in a breath, calming her rattled nerves, then pressed redial.

When the phone connected and she spoke, Sam's irate voice flew through the line.

"Sam, please listen," Hannah said.

"What's wrong? You don't understand English?"

"Jack abducted JJ, and I'm afraid—"

"JJ's his kid. He has every right. Quit bothering me. You and the police. Don't call again."

Hannah's head resounded when Sam slammed the phone in her ear. She stared at the receiver, then hung up and pressed her face in her hands. "Think. Think."

Chapter Sixteen

"Thanks," Andrew said, shaking hands with church members. "We appreciate your prayers."

Hannah stayed close to his side, her eyes wide, as people she knew and those she didn't know came by to offer their thoughts and prayers.

"Have you heard anything?" Jemma asked, hurrying toward them with her two children in tow. Philip wasn't far behind her.

"Nothing," Hannah said. "I'm sick. It's been a week. I've heard nothing. He's trying to scare me. That's how he does things."

A frown marred Jemma's smooth forehead. "I can't even fathom how someone could be like Jack."

Philip's eyes filled with sympathy. "The man is a maniac, but he's not alone. We've all heard of parents kidnapping their children."

He and Jemma shook their heads as if not knowing what else to say until Jemma leaned over and kissed Hannah's cheek. Andrew's heart lifted at the love he saw in his brother's and Jemma's faces.

"Thanks," Andrew said. "I'm working for a while this afternoon, but I'm going to Hannah's later, and I'll call if we learn anything new."

As they moved off, Andrew took Hannah's hand, moving toward the door. He saw so many people eyeing her, giving a nervous wave as if they wanted to say something but didn't have the words. Today the gossip had subsided and the looks were different. Today everyone's eyes were full of compassion. Andrew knew in a small town word got around, and most everyone knew of Hannah's plight.

A woman Andrew had never met sidled up to them and laid her hand on Hannah's. "I'm so sorry about your son, and now you have the little one coming. I wish we had known that…" Andrew saw her glance at him with the look of humility. "You've been so wonderful to support Hannah. We didn't know that…" Her voice trailed off as if she had no idea how to put her thought into words, no idea how to apologize for her earlier accusations about Hannah's pregnancy.

"Thanks," Andrew said, pleased at least that she'd admitted her fault.

"Jenni must have been at work," Hannah whispered. "I'm sure she spoke her mind to some of the gossips."

Andrew squeezed her hand. "People aren't all bad. They just latch on to something that goes against their morals, and they can't let go. Naturally they assumed—" He didn't need to finish the sentence. He and Hannah both knew what some people had assumed.

"I'm not going to hold grudges," Hannah said. "I just thank God for their prayers."

Andrew clutched her arm until they reached the outdoors. "I have to work for a while today. You know that."

"I'll be okay. Jenni said she'd drop by, and I'm sure Claire will visit, too. She was wonderful again last night. She was so supportive and prayed with me. This past week has been so difficult."

"I know. I wish I could make it go away."

"But you can't." Hannah patted his arm. "You've been here for me in every way."

"Please take it easy today. You've been under too much stress, and the baby's due in another six weeks."

"It's hard to take it easy when I'm losing my mind." She squeezed his hand. "Thinking isn't hard. I'll do that. I need time to weigh what we talked about on the way to church this morning."

Andrew slipped his arm around her shoulder. "You mean where Jack might have gone with JJ?"

She nodded. "I'm praying there's someplace he's mentioned—some location that would be a possible hideout. I sense he's nearby since he wants me back. He won't go too far away."

"Let's hope the police have a lead. We'll call when we get home, or maybe there'll be a message."

They hurried across the parking lot, their feet crunching the dried leaves drifting from the oaks and maples. Autumn. Winter. The thoughts rolled through Andrew's mind again. An ending and a new beginning. This horrible time had to end soon, and he and Hannah, God willing, would have their new beginning.

JJ's image shot into his mind and the new baby on the way. God could move mountains. The Lord could raise the dead and count hairs on heads. *Heavenly Father, you know where JJ is. Please help us. Hannah deserves a good life, one without sorrow and fear. Please give her that. I love her more with each beat of my heart.*

Andrew's chest nearly burst with pride as he gazed at Hannah walking by his side. Her brown curls glistened with red in the morning sun, and Hannah's pale skin set off her hazel eyes flecked with gold. His gaze traveled to her rounded belly, and he longed to kiss the bulge that was baby. Hannah's baby. *Their* baby. Andrew gave no credence to the sick man who would harm Hannah. *He* would be the father, not in blood, but in love.

Hannah hung up the phone, her second call to the police since Andrew had left. "They've still heard nothing," she said. She looked at Jenni's tense expression and knew she was also stressed. "The detective said JJ's photograph is everywhere. They're looking, but Jack's vanished."

"They'll find him," Jenni said.

"But it's been a week. I figured they'd find Jack right away if he went home or from his license number. Jenni, he's lugging my son around, and I know JJ doesn't want to be with him. He's afraid. I'm so distressed."

"Someone will recognize him, Hannah."

"They've even put a tracer on my phone, but nothing. Why is he doing this to JJ? He's just a little boy."

"He wants you, Jenni. It's the only way he knows how to get to you."

"He hates me that much?"

"No, he wants to control you that much."

A ragged sob tore from Hannah's throat. "I want to do something." She slapped the kitchen counter, and the sting resonated in her palm.

Jenni rose from her chair and knelt at Hannah's feet. "I know you've prayed, but let's pray together."

Hannah bowed her head as Jenni asked the Lord to lead the authorities to her child. "And give Hannah strength, Lord. Give her courage, and if it's Your will, give her a clue, something that will help the police locate Jack and JJ. Amen."

Hannah echoed her amen and lifted her head. "Thanks, Jenni. You've been a dear friend. Everyone's been kind. Claire came to visit after Andrew dropped me off from church and then Annie called. You've all been so wonderful."

"No thanks necessary. You'd be praying for me if I was in your shoes."

Hannah released a lengthy sigh.

Jenni frowned and stood with her. "Are you okay?"

"Just tired. Weary. Miserable. I can hardly bear the tension. I try to convince myself JJ will be fine. Then I think of Jack's unstable behavior, and I don't know. I need to think. Somewhere in my memory I must know something that will give me an idea."

"Hannah, don't stress yourself. I'm going to go and you should take a nap. Rest. The baby's due soon, and this is a difficult time."

"You should know. Look at you." She followed Jenni into the kitchen.

Jenni grinned rubbing her hand across her protruding belly. "We make great bookends."

Hannah laughed for the first time in days.

Jenni walked to her side, embraced her and kissed her cheek. "Now, listen to me. Rest. I'll talk to you later." She turned, gave a wave and headed for the door.

Hannah closed the door and stood a moment, as her thoughts spun. The same question battered her mind— Where had Jack taken JJ? Her call to Sam had been more than disappointing. She knew no one else to call. Nothing.

The telephone pierced the silence, and Hannah jumped at the sound. She hurried across the room to answer it, and her heart stopped when she heard his voice.

"Where are you, Jack? What do you want?"

"You know what I want. I've given you a week to take my offer. Call off the bloodhounds and be my wife or I'll take JJ so far away you'll never see him."

"You don't want me, Jack. You just want someone to batter around." The words flew out before she could stop them. JJ. She feared for her child. "Is JJ okay?"

"For now."

For now. No. He couldn't mean it, but she didn't want to challenge him. He was trying to frighten her. "Listen to reason, Jack. Please get on with your life, and let me get on with mine. It's too late for us, but you can start again. You have women falling all over you. You don't need me."

"But I want you, Hannah."

No. No. He didn't want her. He wanted… Andrew's offer dropped into her mind. Money. Would that sway him? "Jack, do you want money? I could borrow some money so you can go away. How much do you want? Give me JJ, and I'll give you what I can." It was useless. He'd never give up. Why had she mentioned it?

"So, the rich boyfriend wants to pay me off. That's too easy, Hannah. You'd have JJ and your boyfriend, and what would I have?"

"Money to…" The words ran dry. She already knew money wouldn't stop him. He wanted to make her suffer.

"I'm hanging up. This is your last chance to make a decision. If you want to see JJ again, you're going to have to prove to me that you've called off the police and you're willing to be my wife. What happens next rests on your shoulders. I'll call you very soon, but next time, I want an answer."

The phone slammed in her ears.

Her knees buckled as she sank into a chair. She clung to the resounding silence, turning his words over in her mind. What happened next rested on her shoulders.

JJ. Where would Jack hide him? Since he needed money and wanted Hannah, he would probably hide somewhere close. She sat a moment to get control of her nerves, then returned to the telephone. She had pinned the detective's phone number beside it, and she punched it in. When the detective picked up, she told him about Jack's call, then hung up and leaned against the wall, praying they could trace it.

She tried to picture where Jack might be. Her head pounded with a growing headache. Think. Her thoughts rolled. Picture where Jack... Picture. Her heart lurched.

Photograph albums. Early in their relationship she'd taken pictures of Jack and later of Jack and JJ. She sped to her bedroom, reached to the top closet shelf and pulled down the book of snapshots. She'd wanted to tear up every picture of Jack, but she'd kept them for JJ. Though Jack hadn't been a good father, the boy deserved to have photographs of him.

As she turned toward the living room, the phone rang again. Anxiety mounted as she hurried to lift the receiver, but disappointment flooded her as she listened to the detective.

"But I don't understand. Why can't you trace the call?"

"He used a cell phone. They're harder to trace. The signal comes from the nearest base station tower. That leaves too much area to cover. I'm sorry."

"So am I." Sarcasm knotted her voice.

"We'll find him. The bulletin is out. Sometimes it takes two or three weeks. You have to let us do our job."

And sometimes it takes forever. She thanked him and hung up, frustrated and discouraged. Let them do their job? But what if they couldn't? She knew finding Jack wouldn't be easy, but they had all the technical skills. Why couldn't they trace the call? Why couldn't they find JJ?

Her heart heavy, she carried the album into the living room, sank onto the sofa, and opened the cover. Their few wedding snapshots turned her stomach. Jack had gotten drunk, and he'd been rough with her that night.

Next she flipped past a group of his friends at a bowling alley, a New Year's Eve party when Jack had been drunk again. She turned the page, and tears welled in her eyes. JJ as a newborn. She ran her index finger over his tiny face, his eyes closed, his diminutive fingers curled into his palm.

Brushing away the tears, Hannah paused to calm herself. Think. She turned the page. Jack with a rifle. Jack and a buddy standing by a felled deer. A cabin in the woods—his friends. The photos jarred her thoughts. She hadn't taken the pictures, but someone had, and she'd put them in the album. Where had that been? Not far, she recalled. Private property just off the National Forest. He'd taken her there once, wanting to price out property to buy. She'd gone along knowing he couldn't afford it.

Where had it been? She closed her eyes, trying to picture the day they'd driven there. It had been near a little town with an unusual name. A long shot, but that's the only thought that came to her. She slid the album onto the sofa and headed for the kitchen. From her junk drawer, she pulled out a map of Michigan.

After spreading the map on the kitchen table, Hannah sat and stared at it. It had been north of Loving. They'd passed Hoffmaster State Park. She moved her finger to the Manistee National Forest. It had been south of there, she remembered. Her gaze followed State Highway 37 and the town of White Cloud. They'd stopped there for gas, then made a turn. She scanned the map right, then left.

Hannah's pulse escalated. Jugville. That was it. That was the town with the funny name. Jack had said it had probably been named after moonshine bootleggers.

She eyed the clock. Four. Andrew would be off work in another hour, but she couldn't wait. She needed a good hour to get there, and night fell earlier in late October. If she wanted to find the cabin, she needed light.

Call the police, her logic told her, but she knew her vague remembrance would get them nowhere. The police were too busy for wild-goose chases. But if she located the cabin, if she found Jack and JJ there, then they would believe her and help her.

Hannah darted into her bedroom, slipped on sturdy shoes and a jacket over her knit top. Her hands trembled as she pulled her car keys from her shoulder bag, looked inside for the cell phone—that she so rarely used—then slung her bag over her shoulder.

Outside the apartment, she locked her door, then hurried to her car. The sun had already lowered in the sky, and she couldn't waste time. She slid into her car, started the ignition, and pulled out to the street.

Hannah kept watch on her speedometer as she drove through Grand Haven and Ferrysburg. When she approached Muskegon Heights, she watched for the highway sign and made a left. This route was the quickest route to Highway 37 that she knew.

Andrew slid into her thoughts. Today she needed his strength and confidence, but he wouldn't have allowed her to go. She knew that. She pressed her hand against the child in her belly. The baby rolled and kicked, so full of precious life.

As she drove, reality settled over her. She couldn't go without telling Andrew. He would panic when he didn't find her home, and he'd promised to come to the house after work. She wouldn't frighten him like that. Hannah reached into her bag and pulled out her cell phone, then punched in his office number.

Andrew's voice mail kicked in. "Andrew, don't be angry," she said. "Jack phoned. The police couldn't trace the call, but I have an idea where JJ might be. I'll call you as soon as I know for sure. I won't do anything foolish. Promise. I'll leave the cell on, and you can call me when you get this message. I love you, Andrew."

She lingered with the feeling of *I love you* on her lips. Three tiny words, yet so powerful. So meaningful. The love of a man and woman. God's love. So powerful. She disconnected, checked the power button, then slipped the phone in her jacket pocket.

The heavy line of trees shrouded the late-afternoon sun, and as the forest deepened, Hannah felt alone and frightened. Maybe she'd been foolish to leave without Andrew. A pain charged through her, and she pressed her hand against her stomach as a spasm surged low in her belly. She'd been under too much stress, too much turmoil.

When she drove into White Cloud, a filling station appeared on her left. If her memory was correct, Jack had stopped there on the drive to the cabin. Her mind stretched back to the occasion. Which way had they turned after they left the station? Right or left? Undecided, her gut instinct was to make a right turn, heading east. She did and followed the gloomy road, watching the sun approach the horizon through her rearview mirror. She would never find the cabin once it got dark.

The farther she traveled, the more her confidence faded. Should she have turned west instead of east? The highway seemed too well-traveled. Too straight. She pulled to the shoulder, tears blurring her vision. Her back throbbed with a low, dull ache and another cramp rolled through her abdomen. She lowered her head against the steering wheel, praying God would give her fortitude. She had no confidence in which direction to follow.

Andrew pulled away from Bay Breeze, his mind heavy with concerns. The day had been filled with problems—over-booking, a laundry snafu and a resort packed with overeager guests visiting the area to enjoy the autumn colors. But his greatest worry was JJ. When he hadn't been solving problems at the resort, he'd been praying for the boy's safety. His chest ached for Hannah. After he'd brought her home from church, she'd been devastated when the police had had nothing to report.

He hadn't talked with her since, and he'd meant to call. He pulled out his cell phone, punched in her number, then listened to it ring. No answer. Concern prickled along his spine. She wouldn't leave home without letting him know.

He shook the fear from his head. She'd probably gone to visit Jenni or maybe Jemma. Claire might have invited her for dinner. Yet she'd said she didn't want to leave the house. He didn't know her friend's phone numbers offhand, and he wished he'd called her before he'd left the resort. He faltered. Hannah might have called the office. He'd forgotten to check his voice mail before he'd checked out for the day.

Rifled by concern, Andrew pulled out his cell phone and hit the buttons to retrieve his desk messages. He was probably being ridiculous, but with Jack loose and holding JJ, Andrew could never be sure what the lunatic might try next.

When he heard Hannah's voice, he felt relieved until he heard her message. His heart stopped. She'd gone out alone to find Jack. He slammed his fist against the steering wheel. Why would she do that? Independence. Stupid independence. She was endangering herself and the baby for the sake of doing it alone. Frustrated and fearful, Andrew reviewed her call and memorized her cell phone number, then pressed the buttons. Three rings, four, then Hannah's voice.

"Where are you?" he yelled before he could stop himself.

"I don't know for sure. I think I made a wrong turn."

"Hannah, don't be foolish. Come home. I'll go with you."

"It's getting dark, Andrew. I have to find JJ. I'm going to check the cabin, and then I'll call you if he's there. I won't let Jack see me."

"It's too dangerous." He clenched the cell against his ear, wishing he could wring her beautiful neck. "Hannah, I love you. Please, come back. Don't do this."

"I have to. I need to go the other direction, I think. I'm close. Please don't ask me to stop now."

He understood. JJ was her child. Any mother would fight to find her child, but she needed protection, and he longed to be there for her.

"Where are you headed?"

"Jugville."

"Jugville? Where's that."

Trying to comprehend through the static, Andrew listened to her instructions and tried to calculate the location without a map. The Manistee National Forest, a town called Jugville. The more he thought the more perplexed he became. Why? Why? Why?

"I'm heading your way now, Hannah. I'll find you. Don't do anything foolish. You have an unborn child to protect, too. Don't take any chances."

With Hannah's unconvincing promise in his ears, he disconnected. She'd already gone too far. Going off without thinking put her, JJ and the baby in danger if Jack went berserk.

Immediately Andrew made a speedy call to the police and relayed what Hannah had done and where she was headed. When he hung up, he stepped on the accelerator and headed up Highway 31, his fingers clenching the steering wheel. Dusk already hung against the treetops. In the national forest, Hannah would face the dark early.

Worse, she might face Jack. He pressed his foot against the accelerator again.

Hating the time she'd lost, Hannah eased her back against the seat as the pain passed. She'd been too tense, too frightened. She tried to calm her thoughts. Just go back, Hannah. It's the other way. You should have made a left not a right. She remembered the road had been winding. Jack had passed a lake or two that day.

She feared disappointment. She'd counted on this location to be the hideout. Jack had nowhere else to turn where the police wouldn't find him. She felt the Lord urging her on.

Getting a grip on her fears, Hannah doubled back. She crossed the White Cloud highway and followed M-20, but again, the highway ran too straight, too populated. White Cloud County Park appeared on her right. She slowed. This wasn't it, either.

What could she do? The gas station struck her thoughts. She would return there and ask directions. She headed back to M-37 and turned right. At the station, she pulled up to the building and ran inside. "Jugville? Which way."

"You make a left just up the road. No traffic light. You'll have to watch for it."

"No traffic light." That had been her mistake. "I'm looking for someone." She dug into her shoulder bag and located JJ's snapshot, then handed it to him.

He stared at the photo with no recollection on his face. He shook his head. "I don't remember. Sorry."

"The boy's five, dark wavy hair. He has a broken left arm."

"Broken arm," the man said. "I didn't recognize the picture here, but the broken arm, I remember. He and a man came in for a couple of pops a few days ago. The boy wasn't happy. Kept whinin' to go home."

JJ. Hannah's heart thundered, and something twisted deep in her stomach.

"You okay?" the man asked.

"I'm fine," she said. "Thank you." She turned to go. "Did the man give you any inkling where they were staying? I really need to talk with him."

"Not that I recall. Sorry."

Hannah stuffed the snapshot back in her handbag. "You said turn left."

"Just a few yards up the road. You'll see it."

"Thanks."

She hurried to the door, praising God for getting her this far. Jack and JJ had been here. She'd asked for guidance, and the Lord had led her here.

Hannah started the car and pulled onto the highway, recalling that she'd seen the turnoff but had mistaken it for a farmer's driveway. Ahead, she saw the road again and, this time, turned left. Dusk enveloped her as she wound her way through the heavy forest. She turned on her headlights and soon saw a small sign tilted toward the ground announcing Jugville city limits.

Hannah's pulse escalated. A small house and shed stood at the left with a late-model car parked nearby, then an unlighted diner with a closed sign in the window. She slowed as she reached the center of town—a few small businesses, a gas station and a grocery store.

Hannah parked in front of the market, grabbed her purse, and headed inside. A bell tinkled as she entered. As her eyes adjusted to the overhead lights, the scent of raw meat, cardboard boxes and dust assailed her.

The clerk rose from a chair behind the counter, dropped his magazine, and peered at her. "What can I do for you?" he asked.

"I'm trying to locate someone." Her hands shook as she searched for JJ's photo in her shoulder bag. "I know they're staying at a hunting cabin around here somewhere."

"There's a couple cabins up the road apiece." He swung his hand to the left. "Most are set back pretty far off the road." He pulled out a handkerchief and blew his nose. "They'll be hard to find, 'specially in this light."

She located the photo and handed it to him.

He shook his head. "Never saw that boy."

"He has a broken arm."

He gave his head another shake. "Not many strangers around her this time of year. We'll see more during deer season."

Groceries. Jack had to have food. "The boy's with a man about five feet eight inches. Dark hair."

"The only stranger I've seen in the past week was a man who robbed me last weekend. He was about medium size. Could be five foot nine or ten. White man. Dark hair, but he had a scarf over his face. I just saw his eyes. Dark, evil eyes. He had a pistol."

She searched the man's face, confused and startled. Could the stranger have been Jack? Jack, a robber? He always needed money. Had he wanted money for food? Or had Andrew been correct? Jack needed money for drugs? "Did you notice which way he went?"

"Sorry. He had me lay on the floor. I work alone here, and I stayed down like he told me. He said count to a hundred. I did."

"Did you notice his car when he pulled up?"

"No, I was in the back stocking canned goods. By the time the police came, the guy was long gone. Not a clue."

She stared at the door in panic. Could it have been Jack? Had he stooped to burglary? "This man has a child with him, so I don't—" So what? Jack could have left JJ at the cabin or left him in the car. Or it could have been someone else. "Thanks for your help."

The bell tinkled when she opened the door, sounding frivolous in contrast to the fear that pounded in her head.

A weapon. If it had been Jack, he had a gun. Would he use it on her or JJ? The question lodged in her mind. God alone knew the answer.

As she walked away from the building, a cold gust of wind sent a shiver down her back. She slipped into the car and flipped on the heater. The police. She needed to call them. She punched in 911 and told them all she knew before she turned on the headlights and pulled back out onto the two-lane road. This was the time deer shot out across the highway and animals crept across the road, hoping to make it to the other side. The only varmint she wanted to locate was Jack.

As Hannah drove, she peered into the shadows between the trees, looking for lights or a sign of people. The road meandered to the left, then the right. Ahead she noticed a rutted driveway. She slowed and looked down as far as she could see. No lights, no vehicles. She continued, traveling slowly, peering into the dark woods. The road made a sharp left, and her memory stirred. She was close. She sensed it.

Ahead she saw another cut into the woods. She slowed, letting her car stop across the path. No cabin was visible, but the lane meant something. Should she venture down it? Should she park here and walk?

Knowing Andrew was on the way, Hannah faltered. She felt so close, but she would wait for him. She pushed her good sense aside. She'd found her way this far, and couldn't stop now.

Andrew. If he was looking for her, he would recognize her car on the road. She pulled out her cell phone, and in the dim light, she pressed in his number.

He answered on the second ring. "Where are you?"

"I'm close. At a gas station just before the turnoff, an attendant remembered a child with a broken arm traveling with a man. I just passed through Jugville and—" She faltered. If she mentioned the gun and the burglary, Andrew would be furious. "And he mentioned some cabins up the road."

"Don't move. Stay in the car. I just turned onto M-37. I'm about thirty minutes behind you. I'll call the police and let them know where you are."

"I called them, Andrew. I'm down the lane from a cabin now, and I sense this is the place."

"Don't move. Do you hear me? I'll be there soon."

"I hear you," she said.

He disconnected, and Hannah dropped the cell phone into her pocket. She sat a moment, examining the path. She'd heard him, but she didn't want to stop. She was so close.

A pain rolled through her belly again, and she released a groan. Hannah placed her hand over her abdomen and stretched her legs forward. The ache eased away, and she unlatched her seat belt, opened the door and stepped outside. She pressed against the door until it clicked.

Maybe standing outside she could relax the cramp. Instead, fear sparked in every vein. Supporting her belly, she crept forward and peered down the gloomy path. The lane was rutted and had enough room for a car to get through. She took a step forward, her legs quaking. This could be nothing or everything. She inched forward, wanting only to see if a cabin was up ahead.

Leaves crunched beneath her feet. A twig cracked with her next step. Each movement sounded like a gunshot in the quiet woods. Her heart thundered in her ears while adrenaline raced through her limbs. If Jack was there, she'd be in danger if he saw her. She halted. She'd promised Andrew to wait for him. Forcing herself back toward the car, she strained to see down the darkened road for a vehicle. Andrew. The police. Someone to help her.

As she touched the door handle, another pain rolled through her belly and down her legs. She leaned against the car, her legs wobbling with the baby's weight and pressure aching in her belly.

When the pain faded, she grasped the door handle, but before she pulled it open, a horrifying awareness shot through her. This was the end of October. The baby was due December tenth. She placed her hand beneath the heavy burden. It couldn't be. Yet reality surged through her, sharpening her senses.

She was in labor.

Chapter Seventeen

Andrew gripped the steering wheel and punched in the police's phone number. "Hannah's in Jugville just outside White Cloud. She said there's no traffic light at the turnoff."

"We already have the state police alerted," the detective said. "Keep us posted."

Andrew agreed and disconnected. He glanced at the cell phone, longing to call Hannah, but afraid of what he'd learn. Andrew had begged her to stay put, not to take chances, but Hannah didn't listen when her determination took over.

Her image filled his head—Hannah in the woods, stumbling through the darkness. He feared for her and the baby. He feared that she might actually have found Jack and that he would do something rash.

Andrew slammed his fist against the steering wheel. Why hadn't she waited for him? The question rang in his mind. He knew the answer.

He could still hear her voice speaking over the static-filled cell phone. "I love you," she'd said. She loved him. She'd admitted it.

Dear Lord, please let them find her and JJ safe. I know I deserve nothing, but You've promised to hear our prayers. Lord, I love Hannah and JJ. I will love the new baby as if it was my own. Father, please keep them safe. Please.

Tears blurred his vision. Tears. He hadn't cried for years until he'd learned what loving meant. He'd hardened his heart against emotion and hurt. But no longer. When he'd learned Hannah was pregnant, he'd asked himself questions. Could he love the child? Could he love a child conceived in violence?

Then he ignored his logic and searched his heart. When he'd felt the child move against his palm and imagined the tiny being growing in Hannah's belly, his attitude had changed. The blessing had become real, and God had given him a chance to share in the joy.

Today Andrew could no longer hide the true love he had for Hannah and her family. She'd brought him out of his lonesome world and made him feel whole and purposeful. Now she'd offered him another gift—love.

As he neared White Cloud, he searched for signs of the police or Hannah's car. A gas station came into view, and he decided it must be the one Hannah had mentioned. Keeping his focus on the left, he recognized the road she'd described, unmarked by a traffic signal. He slowed and turned.

The cell phone remained in his hand, and he itched to call her. He tried to slip it back into his pocket, but couldn't.

His senses bristled. What if she'd done the unthinkable? What if she'd gone to the cabin? The possibility wasn't beyond reason when it came to Hannah.

He eyed the phone again, then slowed along the

winding road to punch in her cell number. He prayed she had followed his plea for once and had stayed in her car until help arrived.

Hannah eased herself onto the car seat and dropped her head against the headrest. Her hands trembled with pain and apprehension. How could she sit there and wait?

She lifted her head and peered down the road. The dusky sky made everything look gray and blurred. Her heart jumped. Had she seen movement? A rise of dust in the distance? Imagination.

Her head dropped back as a contraction surged through her. She closed her eyes and tried to focus on breathing. She counted slowly, unwilling to give way to the pain, unwilling to cry out.

When the pain subsided, anger fired in her. She had to protect JJ and her unborn child. She raised her head, wondering what to do. Go or stay?

She sent a prayer to heaven and clung to the steering wheel to keep herself from leaving the car. She needed to use good sense, but with her son in jeopardy, good sense meant nothing. She peered again into the gloom. Her pulse escalated as a black car neared her, its headlights off and the bubble light on top silent.

She pulled herself together and slid from the seat as the squad car halted and an officer hurried from the car to meet her. "Are you okay?"

"I waited for you," she said. "This might not be the place, but I didn't want to take a chance."

"Smart lady." He looked over his shoulder as another squad car pulled to the side of the road. "Stay here," he said, turning away and heading back to the other officers.

She watched as they pulled rifles from the car and

slipped on what she assumed were bullet-proof vests. From what she could see, they planned to go into the woods on foot. She eyed her watch, wondering where Andrew was and trying to calculate the time since she'd had the last contraction.

Officers moved forward, heading along the fringe of the woods, and her heart thundered, fearing JJ could be harmed in the altercation. She stumbled through the tangled weeds toward one of the officers. "If Jack's there, he has my son. He's only five."

"We'll be on guard. Don't worry." He patted her arm and turned, but a sound slid from her throat as she felt another contraction take hold. Her knees weakened, and she grasped the officer's arm for support.

"Are you sure you're okay?" He eyed her, his focus lowering to her large belly.

"I'm in labor," she said, wanting to stop herself but unable to with the pressure that swept over her.

"Now that's just wonderful," he said, shaking his head.

"I'm sorry," she groaned. "I didn't time it this way."

His look grew tender. "I apologize. It's just that you're right—this isn't good timing. I'll call for an ambulance."

Nothing seemed to be good timing, she thought, remembering how she'd pushed Andrew away when he'd proposed. She realized now how much she'd hurt him with her rejection. "Thank you," she said, praying the ambulance would arrive soon.

The officer hurried to the squad car, apparently to call EMS, then headed down the path following the other officers.

When he'd vanished, she settled into her car, her prayers rising to heaven. She leaned back, allowing her petitions to calm her, but when her cell phone jangled, she jumped, her nerves raw. She dug the phone from her pocket and answered.

"Hannah." Andrew's voice flooded over her.

"The police are here, Andrew."

"Thank God," he said. "Are you all right?"

She took a deep breath. "I've gone into labor."

Panic rose in his voice. "Dearest Lord, no. Hang on, Hannah. I'm close. I've just turned onto Jugville Road."

A noise sounded, and Hannah flinched. "Something's happening, Andrew. I have to go." She pushed the end-call button and slipped the cell back into her jacket pocket.

As she pushed open the car door, a contraction rushed through her, and she let out a groan, trying to conquer the fear and weakness that wracked her. She glanced at her watch. About ten minutes apart.

She couldn't bear the wait. Hannah slid from the driver's seat and stood a moment to get her balance. She gathered her courage and moved forward. With each step her fear grew. She peered into the trees and faltered. Had a light flickered through the branches, or had it been her imagination?

She forced herself to go on. Leaves crackled, twigs snapped, but she pushed aside her panic. If JJ was in a cabin behind those trees, she wanted to know.

She kept her body protected by the thick underbrush, and as she moved forward, the light she'd questioned earlier became real. She stood behind a tree trunk and looked into the clearing. Officers crouched outside the house, and from inside the hum of country music drifted toward her, covering the outdoor sounds she hoped.

The dusk had deepened, and the shadows stretched along the ground. Someone was inside, and she longed to cry out, to call JJ's name, but she clamped her teeth together to keep her silence.

Her focus turned to the police. What would they do? Anything they might try could put JJ in danger. She couldn't bear it.

A flash of light jerked her attention toward the cabin. A lamp had been turned on in a room close to her. The shade was up, and she peered at the window, squinting to see inside. JJ. Her heart leaped. Could she get his attention? Could she signal him to come outside?

Let us do our job. She recalled the officer's comment, a comment she questioned, but they were here, and JJ was inside. A lump formed in her throat, and she glanced at her watch, too dark to see in the woods. She leaned her arm to catch the last of the dusky light. She had three minutes or less before another contraction. She sank to the ground, praying she could control her pain. She had to be there for JJ when he needed her.

Andrew spotted the police cars in his headlights and pulled off the road. Two cars had parked on the grassy shoulder, and he pulled in behind them. Farther up the road, he spotted Hannah's car. He jumped from the sedan and darted toward her, then faltered. She wasn't inside, or was she?

Fear gripped him as he dashed to the driver's window to look. The front and back seats were empty. His pulse pounded in his temple. She wouldn't— Yes, she would, despite his pleading.

Frustration tore through him, mingled with panic. He turned and headed up the path, keeping his body hidden by the trees. The ruts and broken limbs tangled in his feet, and he tripped, catching himself with a tree branch. The rustle of dried leaves sent fear soaring over him. He prayed the police wouldn't think he was Jack.

He strained his eyes into the darkness and finally spotted a light ahead. Shifting farther from the path, Andrew took cover behind a broad tree trunk. Leaning forward, he spotted shadowy silhouettes crouched in the opening in front of the cabin. A rifle glinted in the cabin light.

Why were they waiting? JJ could be dead or injured inside. His heart thudded against his chest, and his stomach knotted with desperation.

Hannah clutched the damp earth, waiting for the pain to pass. She clamped her jaws together, breathing, counting, praying. The contractions were getting closer. Somewhere on the highway an ambulance was on its way, and she'd be safe. But what about her son? What about JJ?

Fear prodded her. She raised herself and peered around the tree to the lighted window. JJ was inside. She crept forward on her knees to the edge of the woods and grasped a piece of broken branch, then waited for the opportune moment. JJ neared the window and she tossed it.

She missed. Hannah's hope sank. She had to lure her son outside. She felt a stone beneath her hand and sent up a prayer. Her courage rising, she lifted it and tossed it toward her son. It met its mark. She heard the tink against the glass, but did Jack hear it too?

JJ turned and moved closer to the window and peered outside. He pressed his nose against the window, but she'd made a mistake. In her excitement, she hadn't thought about the officers. In a heartbeat, he'd vanished from the window. Had JJ seen them? Would he tell Jack?

* * *

Andrew heard a noise. Something had struck the cabin window, and he'd seen JJ looking into the night. Hannah? Had she been that foolish? The answer came without reservation. Yes.

He crouched behind a tree and peered into the darkness. Hannah was there somewhere. He wanted to call to her, but he pressed his lips together, controlling the driving urge.

Instead, he took a step closer to where he suspected she was hidden. A twig snapped beneath his feet, and an officer swung toward him, his rifle aimed at his chest.

Andrew raised his hands above his head. "Don't shoot," he whispered. As an officer bounded toward him, he heard Hannah gasp.

He wanted to run to her, but he stood still trying to explain who he was while his hands fumbled into his pocket for his wallet. The officer studied his ID, then ordered him to get back.

As he retreated into the woods, he spotted Hannah in the throes of a contraction. He hurried to her and grasped her hand, but before he could speak, the cabin door jerked open and a figure leaped from the house. Andrew grasped Hannah's hand. "I'm here, Hannah," he said, but his heart had stopped when she saw Jack held JJ in his arms.

The child sobbed, and Hannah's eyes widened.

"Jack won't hurt him," he promised Hannah, praying the man had an ounce of fatherly love in his heart.

Jack darted toward Andrew's hideout with JJ kicking and wiggling in his arms. The officer yelled, and when he didn't stop, a warning shot rang out. With his heart in his throat, Andrew blocked the view from Hannah.

Jack's footsteps thudded past as Hannah's body relaxed, and her grip lessened.

"I waited like I promised, but I'm afraid for the baby," she whispered.

"Don't be afraid. I love you, Hannah."

The police hesitated, and Andrew knew they feared for JJ's safety. Another shot pinged against the dirt, and Hannah jerked upward. "JJ," she cried.

"He'll be fine, Hannah. Just keep praying."

Andrew heard a motor race and turned to see a car shoot out of the woods heading toward the officers. But in the flash of the headlights, Andrew caught sight of JJ running from the woods where Jack had hidden the car.

"He's safe, Hannah. Jack let him go."

Hannah clung to him, praising God, and Andrew bent to kiss her hair before he rose and ran toward JJ.

One officer headed for the boy while another's footsteps sounded in the gravel, racing down the lane toward the highway. Tires squealed from the road.

JJ dashed into Andrew's arms, tears rolling down his cheeks.

"You're okay, pal," Andrew said, barely able to say the words without releasing a sob.

Fearful, Andrew shifted his gaze toward Hannah. "We need an ambulance for the boy's mother," he said to the officer. "She's in labor."

The man nodded as if he knew.

Andrew lifted JJ in his arms, and, as he turned, the ambulance pulled into the clearing. Seeing JJ's fearful look, Andrew hugged him tighter. "Your mom's fine, pal. The baby's coming."

"It is?" JJ said, watching the emergency technicians lift her onto a stretcher.

"They'll take your mom to the hospital."

"Can we go, too?"

"We sure can." He hugged the boy to his chest, so aching with love that he could hardly bear it.

Chapter Eighteen

The next day, Hannah lay in bed, her baby daughter in her arms. The Lord had blessed her with a healthy child despite her early arrival. Praising God for the perfect gift, she caressed the baby's translucent skin and ran her finger over her tiny hands.

The nurse arrived and lifted the newborn from Hannah's arms. "Time's up," she said, her voice filled with kindness. "You need to rest."

Hannah understood and watched the nurse lower her precious daughter into the bassinet and wheel her from the room.

The horrifying experience of the previous day rolled through her mind over and over. Andrew's frantic look, JJ's fright, the uncontrollable pain, all seemed an endless nightmare, yet God had heard her cries for help.

"How are you?"

Andrew's voice drew Hannah's attention to the doorway, and she smiled. "Alive and well."

"The baby's beautiful. And I can see already she's a sweet little girl who'll look just like her mama. I still can't believe it."

"What did JJ say when you told him? I bet he wanted a brother."

Andrew strode toward her, carrying a huge floral arrangement. "JJ said he loves you, and he'll get used to his new sister."

Hannah chuckled while contentment washed over her. "He's a good boy, Andrew."

"He is good, just like his mom." Andrew placed the flowers on her bed stand, bent down, and kissed her forehead before placing his lips against hers. "I stopped by the nursery before I came here. They'd just wheeled her in. She looks so fragile yet she's healthy. Six pounds, two ounces. Amazing. I praise God for that. I was so afraid…"

"Me, too," she said. "I would never have gone after Jack if I'd known what was going to happen."

"You should never have gone anyway because the man who loves you asked you not to go." He pulled the chair closer and sat beside her. "If I'd lost you, Hannah, I don't know what I would have done."

Witnessing the pain in his face, she lowered her eyes. "I'm sorry that I hurt you, but I had to go. I had to find JJ before Jack did something unspeakable."

"Hannah."

The tone of his voice jerked her to attention, and she looked into his serous eyes. "What is it?"

"The police contacted me last night. Jack's dead."

"He's dead?" The news surged over her like a

wave, yet rolled back in a calming relief. "What happened?"

"In the chase, he lost control and crashed into a tree. He died immediately. They found drugs in the car."

She couldn't speak, and as the ragged breath left her, Hannah realized for the first time in many years she was free. "It's over then."

"It's over."

She lifted her eyes and let her gaze settle on Andrew's handsome face. She understood his pain, she understood his mistakes, and she trusted him with her life. She'd made mistakes of her own. Andrew had taken her and her family into his world as if they were special, and she finally understood that they were. "I love you, Andrew. I can't tell you enough how sorry I am to have refused your proposal. Life seemed so devastating, and I had been so confused."

He pressed his index finger against her lips. "I know, and I haven't given up. You've said you love me. I've loved you so long. I cherish JJ and that beautiful little girl without a name. I want to marry you, Hannah, and I'm willing to wait."

Her pulse skittered. "You'll still have me?"

"Have you? Life would be empty without you."

Tears rolled down her cheeks, as she saw the look in his eyes.

"And my life would be empty without you."

He reached into his pocket and pulled out a small square box. "I've carried this with me since the day I first proposed, Hannah, just waiting for you to accept."

Her hands trembled as she lifted the lid and saw the

lovely ring inside. Four diamonds sparkled against the yellow gold. Her heart swelled as joy and thankfulness filled her. "It's beautiful."

He took the box from her and slid the ring onto her finger. "The four stones represent the four of us. It seemed fitting."

The four of us. The beautiful words drifted over her like cherry blossoms. Andrew's eyes glinted brighter than the gems, and Hannah knew her joy was complete. God had answered every prayer and given her even more than she could have asked.

"We have one last piece of business," Andrew said, clutching her hand.

"Business?"

"Our little daughter needs a name."

"Hope," Hannah said. "I've been thinking how hope has been what kept me trying to make sense out of my life. I read a verse in Romans 5 recently that made my heart leap when I read it. 'And hope does not disappoint us, because God has poured out his love into our hearts by the Holy Spirit, whom he has given us.' God's love hasn't disappointed us."

Andrew's gentle look melted over her. "We have our faith, our love, and now our little daughter Hope. What could be better?"

Hannah looked into his tender gaze. "Nothing. Nothing at all."

Hannah stood at the back of the church, amazed at the number of people who'd come to their wedding. The church had been adorned with autumn colors and banners depicting the harvest. Her bouquet echoed the seasonal theme with gold Fuji mums, russet asters and apricot-tinted carnations adorned with autumn leaves, and she'd chosen a simple gown in the softest beige.

She scanned the guests, touched by their friends and church family's compassion and love—Jenni and Todd, Annie and Ken, Jemma and Philip, Esther and Ian Barry from Bay Breeze, Christie Hanuman and her husband Patrick from the congregation, Claire, even Carla sat near the front, her face beaming. Hannah had entrusted tiny Hope, who was blossoming with good health, to Annie.

The bridal music sounded, and joy filled Hannah's heart as she glided down the aisle to meet Andrew. He waited for her up front, dressed in a dark suit with a boutonniere in his buttonhole, looking so handsome and so strong.

Thanksgiving had been two days earlier, and today she had so much for which to be grateful. When she reached Andrew, they joined hands and made a promise to God and to each other that they would love and honor each other through eternity.

The diamond ring sparkled on her finger, each stone so special, so significant—Andrew, JJ, Hope and Hannah. Love abounded, and when the pastor pronounced them husband and wife, she faced Andrew and rejoiced in his deep, cherished kiss.

JJ came forward, and Andrew lifted Hope from Annie's arms. They stood facing the people she'd grown to love and felt as if God had blessed her beyond measure.

The pastor's final blessings filled the room. "As you leave here today, keep this moment in your hearts. Remember God's Words in First Corinthians. `And now these three remain: faith, hope and love. But the greatest of these is love.' Hannah and Andrew, JJ and baby Hope, go with God's blessing."

Andrew looked at her, his smile brighter than the sun, and she heard his murmur in her ear. "Faith, hope and love."

They were three of the most beautiful words Hannah had ever heard.

* * * * *

Dear Reader,

This letter is bittersweet. We're saying goodbye to Loving, Michigan, and all its residents. I've enjoyed writing the seven novels that were set in the imaginary town on the shores of Lake Michigan, patterned after the real city of Grand Haven.

I ended the series with Andrew Somerville, the prodigal son who returned to Loving after wasting his inheritance. His journey demonstrates God's forgiveness and the forgiveness we share with one another. Yet, the Lord says to forgive as we want to be forgiven, and that includes our own sinful nature.

Hannah's struggle with domestic violence is all too familiar to us in this difficult world. I encourage all of us to support women's shelters and to be watchful for signs from family, friends or neighbors who are living a life of fear and abuse. Let us keep the shelters and their occupants in our prayers, asking God for their peace and safety in an often frightening world.

Remember Jesus' words in John 16:33. "In this world you will have trouble. But take heart! I have overcome the world."

May God bless each of you.

Gail Gaymer Martin

If you liked the Faith on the Line *series
from Love Inspired, you'll love the*
Faith at the Crossroads *series,
Coming in January from Love Inspired Suspense!*

And now, turn the page for a sneak preview of
A TIME TO PROTECT *by Lois Richer,
the first instalment of* Faith at the Crossroads.

On sale in January 2006 from Steeple Hill Books.

Brendan Montgomery switched his beeper to vibrate and slid it back inside his shirt pocket. Nothing was going to spoil Manuel DeSantis Vance's first birthday party—and this large Vance and Montgomery gathering—if he could help it.

Peter Vance's puffed out chest needed little explanation. He was as formidable as any father proudly displaying his beloved child. Peter's wife Emily waited on Manuel's other side, posing for the numerous photographs Yvette Duncan insisted posterity demanded. Apparently posterity was greedy.

Judging by the angle of her camera, Brendan had a hunch Yvette's lens sidetracked from the parents to the cake she'd made for Manuel. Who could blame her? That intricate train affair must have taken hours to create and assemble and little Manuel obviously appreciated her efforts.

"Make sure you don't chop off their heads this time, Yvette." As the former mayor of Colorado Springs, Frank Montgomery had opinions on everything. And as

Yvette's mentor, he'd never been shy about offering her his opinion, especially on all aspects of picture-taking. But since Yvette's camera happened to be the latest in digital technology and Frank had never owned one, Brendan figured most of his uncle's free advice was superfluous and probably useless. But he wouldn't be the one to tell him so.

"Don't tell me what to do, Frank," Yvette ordered, adjusting the camera. "Just put your arm around your wife. Liza, can you get him to smile?" Satisfied, Yvette motioned for Dr. Robert Fletcher and his wife Pamela, who were Manuel's godparents, and their two young sons, to line up behind the birthday boy.

Brendan eased his way into the living room and found a horde of Montgomery and Vance family members lounging around the room, listening to a news report on the big screen television.

"Alistair Barclay, the British hotel mogul now infamous for his ties to a Latin American drug cartel, died today under suspicious circumstances. Currently in jail, Barclay was accused of running a branch of the notorious crime syndicate right there in Colorado Springs. The drug cartel originated in Venezuela under the direction of kingpin Baltasar Escalante, whose private plane crashed some months ago while he was attempting to escape the CIA. Residents of Colorado Springs have worked long and hard to free their city from the grip of crime—"

"Hey, guys, this is a party. Let's lighten up." Brendan reached out and pressed the mute button, followed by a chorus of groans. "You can listen to the same newscast tonight, but we don't want to spoil Manuel's big day with talk of drug cartels and death, do we?"

His brother Quinn winked and took up his cause.

"Yeah, what's happened with that cake, anyway? Are we ever going to eat it? I'm starving."

"So is somebody else, apparently," Yvette said, appearing in the doorway, her flushed face wreathed in a grin. "Manuel already got his thumb onto the train track and now he's covered in black icing. His momma told him he had to wait 'til the mayor gets here, though, so I guess you'll just have to do the same, Quinn."

Good-natured groans filled the room.

"Maxwell Vance has been late since he got elected into office," Fiona Montgomery said, her eyes dancing with fun. "Maybe one of us should give him a call and remind him his grandson is waiting for his birthday cake. In fact, I'll do it myself."

"Leave the mayor alone, Mother. He already knows your opinion on pretty much everything," Brendan said, sharing a grin with Quinn.

"It may be that the mayor has been delayed by some important meeting," Alessandro Donato spoke up from his scat in the corner. "After Thanksgiving, that is the time when city councilors and mayors iron out their budgets, yes?"

"But just yesterday I talked to our mayor about that, in regard to a story I'm doing on city finances." Brendan's cousin Colleen sat cross-legged on the floor, her hair tied back into the eternal ponytail she favored. "He said they hadn't started yet."

Something about the way Alessandro moved when he heard Colleen's comment sent a nerve in Brendan's neck to twitching, enough to make him take a second look at the man. Moving up through the ranks of the FBI after his time as a police officer had only happened because Brendan usually paid attention to that nerve. Right now it was telling him to keep an eye on the tall, lean man named Alessandro, even if he was Lidia Vance's nephew.

There was something about Alessandro that didn't quite fit. What was the story on this guy anyway?

A phone rang. Brendan chuckled when everyone in the room checked their pockets. The grin faded when Alessandro spoke into his. His face paled, his body tensed. He murmured one word, then listened.

"Hey, something's happening! Turn up the TV, Brendan," Colleen said. Everyone was staring at the screen where a reporter stood in front of City Hall.

Brendan raised the volume.

"Mayor Vance was apparently on his way to a family event when the shot was fired. Excuse me, I'm getting an update." The reporter lifted one hand to press the earpiece closer. "I'm told there may have been more than one shot fired. As I said, at this moment, Maxwell Vance is on his way to the hospital. Witnesses say he was bleeding profusely from his head and chest, though we have no confirmed details. We'll update you as the situation develops."